Señora Rodríguez and Other Worlds

A book in the series

Latin America in translation

En traducción

Em tradução

Sponsored by the Duke–

University of North Carolina

Joint Program in

Latin American Studies

Señora Rodríguez and Other Worlds

Martha Cerda

Translated from the Spanish

by Sylvia Jiménez Andersen

Duke University Press

Durham and London 1997

Translation of the books in the series Latin America in Translation / En Traducción / Em Tradução, a collaboration between the Duke–University of North Carolina Joint Program in Latin American Studies and the university presses of Duke and the University of North Carolina, is supported by a grant from the Mellon Foundation.

Printed in the United States of America on acid-free paper ∞
Typeset in Galliard by Keystone Typesetting, Inc.
Library of Congress Cataloging-in-Publication Data appear on the last printed page of this book.

Acknowledgments

Special thanks to the following people:

Don Joaquín Díez Canedo Mortiz, Joaquín Díez Canedo Flores and Aurora Díez Canedo Flores, publishers of the first edition of *La señora Rodríguez y otros mundos* in Spanish: Editorial Joaquín Mortiz, Mexico, 1990.

Milagros Palma, director of Indigo & Côté-femmes Éditions, the publisher of *La señora Rodríguez et autres mondes*, Paris, 1993.

Luis Mario Cerda, publisher of the second edition of *La señora Rodríguez*, La Luciérnaga Editores, Guadalajara, 1994.

To theater directors, Gerardo Maldonado, Sergio Lasso, Dr. Juan Hernández-Senter, and actresses María Elena Saldaña and Irma Lozano, who brought *La señora Rodríguez y otros mundos* to stages in Mexico City, Guadalajara, Monterrey, and Long Beach, California.

To Sylvia Jiménez-Andersen, the translator.

To Laura Dail and Duke University Press, who made this English-language edition of *La señora Rodríguez* possible.

Contents

I

Señora Rodríguez reached into her purse with her left hand searching for a Kleenex and grabbed a half-licked lollipop. "The drops!" she shouted, "I forgot to give Carlitos his drops," and, sighing, she clasped her hands together before reaching into her purse again, this time with her right hand, and took out a comb, which reminded Señora Rodríguez that she had to dye her hair because she was going to have a party the following Saturday. "How time flies, it seems like only yesterday my niece Laurita was born, and now she's about to turn fifteen. It's too bad her mother died and that shameless brother of mine went, in less than a year, and remarried, that . . ." And saying this, she went back to groping through her purse without any luck. Something became entangled in her fingers, and she pulled out the sandalwood rosary that her mother-in-law had brought her from Rome, with a papal blessing. "What could the good lady, may she rest in peace, have been thinking—but she did not like me at all, as if her son were going to be her mama's boy forever. And me so foolish: Yes ma'am, no ma'am, while she told me what her son should eat, what time he should go to bed, and I don't know how many other things." Señora Rodríguez put her rosary away and pulled out a crumpled paper. "The phone bill!" Señora Rodríguez shouted and ran to her car and headed for the nearest phone company office. "That's all I need, to have my phone disconnected and be cut off from the world; I hope I get there on time.

It's my only source of pleasure besides TV," groaned Señora Rodríguez while she parked her car in a no-parking space. She was about to get out of the car when she heard, "Your license, please." Señora Rodríguez plunged her hand into her purse once again and after taking out some matches, a lipstick, a recipe for bread pudding, a pen without ink and some ancho chiles, she finally found the Kleenex and blew her nose with a loud blast. "Your license, please," repeated the officer. Señora Rodríguez put her dirty Kleenex away and continued searching; her fingers stuck to Susanita's gum. "It's just too much that this kid is so sloppy," Señora Rodríguez complained. "When will she learn not to leave her gum in my purse, what's the officer going to say?" After many tries, Señora Rodríguez was able to pull out Carlitos's report card full of Fs, the rubber bands for Susanita's ponytail and a ten-thousand-peso bill, with which the officer was satisfied. Then Señora Rodríguez remembered that she didn't have a license because she had not passed her driver's exam. When she took the exam she couldn't find her glasses. Naturally, she was carrying the same purse, a gift for her thirtieth birthday from her mother-in-law.

Multiverse

The day I turned one year old, I woke up wet. In their bedroom my parents were snoring after a night of partying three houses down from city hall, where Don Manuel was discussing the new economic program, not with his ministers, but with Columba, his wife, who listened to him, thinking to herself that in a few months she would no longer be the first lady and probably not even a lady, which tormented her, even though deep inside she thanked God, something she had not been able to do in public since Don Manuel had become president. At the stroke of six o'clock in the morning I let out my first scream, feeling abandoned in that house in the same neighborhood in the same city where we all live. The light shone on me from my mama's nightstand. I knew that from that point it would be at least fifteen minutes until I was taken out of my crib, during which time my dad would growl, pulling the blanket up to his eyes and Mama would yawn without waking up completely and Don Manuel would put on a robe to go to the bathroom and Doña Columba would not do anything except dream, probably about her new life. When Mama arrived with my nice dry diapers and my warm bottle and, before changing my diapers, gave me a kiss that tickled my nose, Don Manuel was already phoning his secretary and Doña Columba and Papa were turning over in their respective beds in the same city. However, in London, where it was seven hours later, the queen was peering out discreetly from a balcony in Buckingham Palace and watching an old man off in the distance who wasn't an old man but a disguised guard making his daily rounds as always.

Just like every night, Papa and Mama shook the bed and sighed for a while until they fell asleep, just like Don Manuel and Doña Columba and also the queen and the prince consort. My parents, however, had my sister, who took over my crib, but I, fortunately, could already get out by myself and climb on the bed in another room in the same house in the same city that my sister and I began our lives in and where Don Manuel was finishing his term many kilometers outside of London, where the queen didn't begin or finish anything, since her reign was for life. Therefore, now that I am about to turn twenty, the queen continues to be the queen even though all the rest have changed, for although Papa and Mama continue to sigh during the night, each one does it on their own, just like Don Manuel and his wife: he in Paris and she in London, where the same queen peers out from the same balcony and sees the same old man who no longer needs to dye his hair gray but continues to guard the same queen that Doña Columba admires while she looks at pictures from twenty years ago, when I was a baby and she was the first lady and met the same queen who now doesn't know her because she is no longer the first lady and certainly not the last, because since the term ended she decided to literally unmask herself and, after having surgery by the best plastic surgeon, she told Don Manuel: "Thanks for everything" and she hit the road and that's what she's still doing.

Also in London, but at number 76 in the Roman District of Mexico City, my grandparents live, my Mama's parents, and in the Naples District my Papa's parents do not live because they're dead, but that's where they lived when I was in thc crib, wet, and Don Manuel was in power and Mama woke up at six in the morning to give me my bottle and at the corner of our house there was corn on the cob being sold from a little cart. At that same corner the Rosas used to live, who were five in all: the papa, the mama, Memo, Paty, and Petra, except Petra lived in the service room and would come down daily to clean and buy groceries and meet with José, our gardener, and then would spend her time talking with him, and Memo's and Paty's mama would scold her because she would show up without the bread or tortillas or anything since she would forget what she went for because she was with José, but *that* she did not forget; until one fine day they took off, and we never again heard the Pedro Infante songs that Petra used to play at full volume beginning at seven in the morning. Memo and Paty continue to live there and they grew up just as we did, except they did so without Petra and we did so without José. Paty and my sister are the same age and Memo and I are not, but in any case we still get along very well, except when we go to the movies and I want to sit with Paty and he with my sister, because we both know why we go. And because of that, we got into a fight once and each of us felt that the world turned with us and with our houses and with the queen of England and with Petra and with our grandparents, the ones who are still alive and the ones who are dead, and Papa and Mama, carrying all the world's burdens. And at that time we realized that the world would continue to turn with our cribs and our beds and our graves, with our grandparents and our parents and our sons and daughters and also with our presidents and our kings and queens and our gardeners. And that Petra would continue to run away with José every day and the queen look through the same window and Pedro Infante sing the same songs in the same service room of the same house in the same city in the same world, which would continue to turn just as we were taught in school.

2

Señora Rodríguez received a purse from her mother-in-law, a gift for her birthday. Señora Rodríguez turned thirty years of age and two of marriage, which made her deserving of Señor Rodríguez's mother's recognition, who, until now, could not resign herself to this undeniable fact: she was not the only Señora Rodríguez in the family. Her idiot of a son duplicated her by marrying her daughter-in-law, thus granting her the same title. However, for the purpose of the present book we shall consider "Señora Rodríguez" the daughter-in-law and not the mother-in-law, if she'll excuse us.

Well then, Señora Rodríguez was touched and took the purse (bought on sale at the Puerto de Liverpool department store) and put her keys, her coin purse, some mint lozenges, and her marriage certificate inside, just in case. She put the latter inside the zippered compartment that most purses usually have. "One never knows," sighed Señora Rodríguez, enumerating all the possibilities that she might have to use the document in order to prove her legitimacy to those who would dare doubt her. "One never knows," Señora Rodríguez sighed again, taking the purse by the handle, passing it up her arm until it rested on her shoulder; the normal position (of the purse), from that day forward, on Señora Rodríguez's physiognomy. There are those who say they would not recognize her without it.

After the Canaries

It's not that I don't want to see you, it's that I can't. Ever since Adela began watching me I close my eyes to hide myself. Adela, with her coarse, shaggy hair, like a crown of thorns, training her eyes on me from the moment I asked her: "How old are you?" and she responded, "Forty." And I could never get away from her again. "Forty?" I would repeat to myself, as I watched her dragging herself through the house, without a sound. Or when I wasn't watching her and she abruptly surprised me when I was naked in my bathroom. "What are you doing there, Adela?" I yelled at her, and she responded: "Nothing, ma'am." And, in fact, she wasn't doing anything. "It's incredible that at your age you are so clumsy, Adela," I scolded her constantly, after she broke a glass or dropped a vase or broke some appliance. She would agree with two words: "Yes, ma'am," accentuating the "yes" with her look.

The tone of my insults gradually increased, without any protest from her. "You are an idiot, Adela, I've never met anyone as stupid as you," until, at the height of my exasperation, I slapped her. She did not react. With my hand still shaking I continued: "See what you've made me do, Adela? Please, leave." Adela didn't move.

The next morning I could no longer reprimand her, nor the next, nor the next. I didn't feel like ordering her around. Nevertheless, everything in the house was in order, thanks to her and in spite of her sunken eyes and her sneering expression and her dark voice — just like her dresses.

"Breakfast is ready," she announced when she saw me in the kitchen about to prepare it. I barely sat down when my coffee was served, and before I finished the last sip, she had my bath ready. I couldn't open a drawer without finding Adela's presence in my things: the clothes were always clean and so meticulously arranged that I didn't dare touch them. The living room, impeccable, was no longer the place where I could sit and listen serenely to music, for fear of messing it up and Adela noticing it. If Adela entered through one door, I exited through another, pushed away by her breath. Then Adela began to make insinuations: "Do you feel ill, ma'am?"; "You look pale today, get some rest"; "You are losing a lot of weight, eat well." And I began to follow her around without her seeing me. When I realized it, we were back where we had started.

Adela woke up at five o'clock every morning, and I could no longer sleep, sensing her footsteps, which sometimes stopped very near my bedroom and other times would fade away until they disappeared in the dawn, forcing me to get up right after her and exclaim, "Adela, Adela," then I felt ridiculous, yet at the same time calmed by her voice behind me, which made me stutter, "Well, has the bread arrived yet, Adela?" She turned away, and I went back down the same hall as always to bed.

Other times, on waking up, the first thing that I recognized was her outline vanishing behind the window and reappearing in the doorway: "Did you sleep well?" she interrogated me, poking in her shallow face like a warning. . . .

"Yes, Adela, thank you, and you?"

She looked over my shoulder, as if she had discovered that as a child I wore dirty underwear and twisted socks, and she would not reply.

Then things began to turn up missing. First it was the milk, and Adela said, after a prolonged "Ma'am," which made me think she would say no more, "they stole the milk."

"Who?" I asked, surprised.

"Someone who is not afraid of God," she said in judgment, terminating her explanation.

Later the plants dried up one by one, and in the end the cat ran away after killing the canaries. Adela and I are the only ones left in the house. Adela hardly eats anything, but she prepares my favorite dishes for me and brings them to my bed, for I am so weak that I no longer get up. Adela doesn't let anyone bother me, not even the doctor. On her own she prepares some herbal brews which she uses to bathe me at midnight every time there is a new moon, and right away she bolts the doors so that the evil spirits can't come in. And it's not that Adela is crazy, I assure you, it's just that she doesn't like to go out except on Sundays, to go to church. It's the only time that she leaves me free, and I am using it to write and ask you to forgive me for not visiting you. I can't, really. You don't know what it's like for me to be sitting in my own urine, waiting for Adela to come and change me. But the poor girl has a right to go to mass; if it weren't for her . . .

3

Señora Rodríguez visited the dentist, who, after checking her from head to toe, congratulated her: she was pregnant. Señora Rodríguez didn't know what to say and said nothing. She put her dental X rays in her purse and left. "I had a feeling," she mumbled between her teeth, "that toothache always hit me at the precise moment, I don't know why I listened to my husband; have that molar pulled out, can't you see that it gets in the way of my inspiration? But, it's the wisdom tooth. . . ." And the consequences weren't long in coming. Most assuredly, it had happened when she fell in the water tank and he took off his clothes to rescue her because she couldn't swim. Or when they climbed the orange tree and between one orange and another . . . , Señora Rodríguez turned pale. What excuse would they give her mother-in-law? She wasn't going to like it, how was she going to accept her son's going around and impregnating a woman? It was inconceivable since she had brought him up so well. It would be shameful.

With guilt written on her face Señora Rodríguez got on a bus and didn't get off until it reached the end of the line, where she took another bus back. Señora Rodríguez spent all afternoon going back and forth, until she found the solution: artificial insemination. That's it, she'd swear to her mother-in-law that it was the result of artificial insemination, and her husband would be free from sin.

Señora Rodríguez's mother-in-law screamed, cried, fainted, and, when she regained consciousness, ordered: "Don't let it happen again." That's how Susanita entered the world.

A Happy Family

Papa had done with us what no one had done with him: loved us, pampered us, played on the bed, splashed in the garden fountain, gave us money, and made each one of us feel that we could not live without him. So now after forty years we are still by his side, letting him love us, pamper us, play with us, give us money, and make us feel that we cannot live alone.

Mama, on the contrary, did exactly what had been done to her: overprotected us, corrected us, and imposed her will on us, making us feel that she couldn't live without us, which was the same thing that Papa did, but with other words. In short, the "not able to live without . . ." gradually enveloped us; some of us revolved around the others, attracting each other, loving each other, irritating each other, more and more intensely, until the day Mama died. She left our lives to the astonishment of all, and we watched her go, sent away by the centrifugal force we had generated in that dizzying revolution. When we lost sight of her we realized that, just as she had foreseen, we could not live without her and that is when we began to die. This has been going on for five years. All of a sudden we felt more childlike, and before doing anything we would wonder what Mama would say. It never occurred to us to wonder what *we* would say, as that would mean offending her. Her clothes were still untouched in the closet, and we were still untouched, watching over each other as she used to do.

Upon Mama's death, I inherited Papa, in receivership until Papa dies, that is to say, as long as Mama allows it, because I am sure that she will come for him at the right time. Yes, because Mama used to take care of him just as she took care of us. How could she abandon him like that, forever? That is why I, as soon as she died, became responsible for taking care of him until I put him back in her hands. It's terrible to think that something might happen to Papa and that I might not be able to turn him over to her just as she had left him to me. Fortunately, up to now everything has gone well, Papa goes on loving us, pampering us, giving us money, and making us feel as if we could not live without him. And more and more I look like Mama; it's possible that in a few years even I will not notice the difference.

Nevertheless, we used to be happy. Papa loved Mama, Mama loved me, I loved my sister, my sister loved Papa and, so, we all loved one another. Papa never made Mama mad. I clearly remember that she did not like motor boats, and Papa never bought her one. On the other hand, she didn't need one, we didn't live on the coast, or next to a river, not even next to a lake, so Mama, who hated to make a fool of herself, was happy not having a motor boat in the middle of the living room. For her part, she tried to make Papa mad so that he would show his strength of character in front of us and we could admire him more. We didn't know what to make of so many demonstrations of love and we did nothing.

The famous incompatibility of personalities was never apparent in our family. Mama spent her time being and Papa doing What better way to adapt to each other?

When I got married, I don't know whether I couldn't live without them, or they couldn't live without me, but the fact is that in less than a year I was divorced, as soon as Toñito was born. He is now fifteen and is also loved, pampered, brought up, and spoiled by us: Papa, my sister, who never wants to get married, and me. Perhaps one day we will be able to reproduce ourselves without need of the opposite sex, only through the love we have for each other. Although recently I saw Toñito devour Papa's picture, almost in a fury. The poor boy must have been hungry. Adolescents are that way, they don't understand how happy they are. The same thing used to happen to us; Mama wanted us to be like her and Papa like him. Finally Uncle Quico won, whom we only knew from a picture, since he had split twenty years before and no one knew of his whereabouts.

One thing sure about Mama was that she was a lot of fun. At parties she used to sing and dance for hours and never tired of applause. Now we've become so bored that, no matter how happy we are, we can't even fake it; and it's like I said earlier, we began to die five years ago. No matter how much effort I put into resembling Mama, Papa misses the Sunday afternoons, in front of the television, with his hands between hers; Mama's somewhat flavorless food that he was by then used to; her voice, her look, her support . . . and every day his sadness increases. And that's why I try to joke, retelling the story of his life to make him laugh, but we end up crying.

4

At the age of one Susanita was exactly like her grandmother. "Marvels of science," the blessed woman would say, contemplating her granddaughter with the fear of being supplanted. "First they usurp my last name, now my physiognomy, no doubt they want to drive me crazy," deduced Señora Rodríguez's mother-in-law when the former, by mistake, caressed her instead of her daughter. "All that's missing is for her to put diapers on me," exclaimed the mother-in-law, running away each time that Señora Rodríguez approached her. Despite the resemblance, Señora Rodríguez took Susanita to have her portrait taken with her organdy dress and her little patent-leather shoes. Señora Rodríguez's mother-in-law bristled: a girl born through artificial insemination did not merit such extravagance. She thought even more poorly of the party with balloons and a clown that her daughter-in-law organized for Susanita, without inviting the grandmother. In response, Señora Rodríguez gave her mother-in-law Susanita's portrait. From that day on, the blessed woman began sucking her thumb, peeing in bed every night, just like the girl, and calling her daughter-in-law "Mama." So Señora Rodríguez took the picture away from her and kept it in her purse, along with a balloon, some party favors from the birthday party, and a prayer to Saint Jude asking God the grace of a good death for her mother-in-law, since it had never occurred to the latter that she was the first test-tube grandmother in the world.

Good Habits

"I've already told you he's not here, come back later."

It had only been three days, and already I missed the knocks on the door followed by a prolonged whistle that substituted for the doorbell, which was too formal for René. I also missed his brown eyes looking up at me, his messy hair, and his Mickey Mouse T-shirt, one side longer than the other. René knocked at any hour and with any excuse looking for Paco. It was not possible to forget him, he always arrived at the least opportune moment. Paco wasn't home that afternoon, and when I told him that René had come, he asked, "Did he leave any message?"

"I'm not sure," I answered. It was the third or fourth time that he'd come, I was busy, perhaps he said something like . . . He already knew the answer and turned away, throwing his baseball cap on the easy chair. I picked it up, covered with dust, a week later. Paco never played baseball or asked about his friend again.

Paco finished high school with top grades; it seemed that he wasn't interested in anything else. However, one morning I caught him reading the big-league scores. I was suddenly hit by the image of René in his anguish of a twelve-year-old asking about Paco. I had never thought about his words, which now rang clearly in my memory: "Tell him that I'm going to live in the United States, and that when I'm big I will be famous like Fernando Valenzuela." Paco began to follow the sports section every day, and even though he appeared not to pay much attention to it I would later find the cut-up newspapers in his room. René had sent a postcard from Minneapolis, and we didn't hear any more about him. The neighborhood continued to change, and the lot where they used to play baseball in the old days had become a shopping center.

Paco attended the university. A few years later he would earn his degree and then get married. Everything would happen normally, with that orderliness in which we are born and we die, without even realizing it, busy going up and down stairs, eating, dressing; there was no reason for things to be different. Paco would have kids, I would be a grandmother, his kids' friends would go to Minneapolis, and . . . The door was open, I had opened it myself when I heard the doorbell. Outside, René's brown eyes looked down on me:

"Good afternoon, ma'am, is Paco home?" he asked me with a subtle accent. The tanned skin and the broad back denoted his occupation.

"I play with the Dodgers, I want to invite Paco to the United States, it's possible that he could work there."

I observed him in silence, finally I answered:

"I'm sorry but no one by the name of Paco lives here. We moved here just a year ago, you must be mistaken."

After dinner, as usual, Paco was reading the sports section.

"I wonder what happened to René?" he said. "Today I thought about him."

"He's probably an office worker in Minneapolis, or perhaps a pilot or a laborer, what does it matter," I concluded, while I washed the dishes just like every other night.

"Yes," agreed Paco, dragging out the sound of the *s*.

5

Susanita had an attack of tonsillitis and Señora Rodríguez one of nausea. Immediately Señora Rodríguez took out her calendar and counted the days: "Forty-five, forty-six," fifty days since her last menstruation. Again, she asked herself, cursing Señor Rodríguez, now what would they come up with? They could explain to her mother-in-law that they had won the baby in a raffle or in a coin toss; no, better not, she couldn't stand games of chance, or superstitions, or . . . that's it, a miracle. They would tell her that the baby was in a basket at the side of the river, just like Moses. Yes, at Lake Xochimilco, to be exact. But her stomach? There was no alternative but to wait; she hoped it wouldn't show too soon. With Susanita she didn't need maternity dresses until the seventh month. "Those artificial insemination kids," her mother-in-law used to say. Except that with the second one the muscles are already flabby . . . "As long as it doesn't look like her," sighed Señora Rodríguez.

Señora Rodríguez began vomiting every morning and eating ice cream every afternoon. In the seventh month, she and Señor Rodríguez convinced her mother-in-law to take a trip to Europe that would last two and a half months, after having concealed Señora Rodríguez for a month at Aunt Clotilde's. Upon returning, Señora Rodríguez's mother-in-law found Carlitos, the putative son of her daughter-in-law and her son, who was strangely identical to him. Señora Rodríguez's mother-in-law brought her daughter-in-law a rosary, which she keeps in her purse, along with one of Carlitos's pacifiers and some condoms. "One never knows," sighs Señora Rodríguez.

The First Time

The cockroaches, every day the cockroaches get bigger and bigger. Before, they used to be tiny and skittish; they would hide when they saw me. But that was before, when I was still getting out of bed. They were cranny-dwelling cockroaches, they would only come out at night, like the whores of my youth. And I despised the cockroaches just like *them,* and I crushed them with my shoe. Shameless creatures, they made fun of me because I walked by them without seeing them, spitting at their feet. And all of them wearing lots of makeup and with their dresses stuck to their naked skin. I hated them as much as the cockroaches; I hated them from corner to corner, from night to night, from cranny to cranny. After a while they began to come out earlier. In plain daylight the cockroaches came out of their nests and the whores out of their brothels. By then I was already walking slowly and they no longer feared me, they would not even move when they saw me limping by in front of them. And there were always more. They no longer appeared on the corners or in their crannies, rather they gathered in pairs, in the middle of the streets, looking for clients, or they crossed my path anywhere at all in the kitchen.

All at once they invaded the second floor, and the whores began to look like young ladies. One of them helped me get off the bus and I did not realize who she was until she gave me her card. When the cockroaches began to look like whores I decided to exterminate them with an aerosol insecticide that only gave me a rash: they kept coming and going at will.

As a result of the rash I was bandaged, and as a result of the bandages, sores appeared and became infected; and as a result of everything I ended up here in the hospital. My roommate is here because of a knife wound inflicted on him by one of those women. He also mocked me the day I told him that I never had anything to do with any of them because sex disgusted me. Since then every time he goes to the bathroom he returns with a triumphant smile, while I struggle in my excrement. Behind him the trained cockroaches follow. On his command they fly over me and the biggest one lands on my paralyzed face and walks all over it. I feel it walking on my sweaty skin, encircling my lips, climbing up my nose to look into my eyes and then plunging into my hair. The others get under the sheets and completely cover my body. Since I became paralyzed they do this every day. I try to scream and I can't, but if I could, no one would listen to me because the nurses are a bunch of blind whores who do not see them. "What cockroaches, let's see, where are they?" They would respond when they heard me scream, "Get them off of me, for the love of God."

This morning I heard that I was dead. A nurse took my pulse and said, "He's dead." I don't know, there is no difference between being dead, or paralyzed with terror. But this is the first time that the cockroaches are entering my open mouth. . . .

6

Carlitos and Susanita fought with each other. Señora Rodríguez spanked them and sent them to bed without dinner. “Impertinent kids, they made me miss the best part of my soap opera.” Señora Rodríguez took out a Tin Larín chocolate from her purse and ate it to remove the bitter taste from her mouth. Everything seemed to be going from bad to worse: Señor Rodríguez did not have a job, she had gained ten kilos, and, to top it off, her mother-in-law was ill. Señora Rodríguez took out some dry-roasted peanuts from her purse and began to eat them one by one. She would have to sell the emerald ring that Señor Rodríguez had given her eight years before for saying that Carlitos had been adopted. But it wasn't the ring that weighed on her, rather those surplus kilos and a lack of energy, which Señora Rodríguez tried to mitigate with chocolates, popcorn, and soap operas, unable to control a slight air of rebellion that shook her already messy hair. And then Señora Rodríguez remembered that in the morning she had bought a shampoo, which was being advertised on television, precisely at that moment, and which was guaranteed to be marvelous. With that Señora Rodríguez cheered up and forgot her husband, her kids and her mother-in-law, imagining the new hairdo that she would show off the following day when she washed her hair. This is what Señora Rodríguez was thinking, putting the last dry-roasted peanut in her mouth and throwing the cellophane bag in the trash, without taking her eyes off the television.

The City of Children

The boy with the red beret put the packages in a bag; then he filled another one and another one until he had filled five big plastic bags, imprinted with the red initial of the supermarket chain they belonged to. The boy also wore an apron, on which his face appeared on an identification card, as if it were peering through an acrylic window. He must have been about ten years old.

Something about him seemed familiar; I didn't know what. Then I remembered when I used to wander through the hospital rooms looking for help. I wasn't sick, but I needed to prove it to myself by seeing true pain and desperation with my own eyes. There I saw for the first time, in the nursery, the section designated for baggers. They were in uniform with their red caps and they weren't crying; their eyes were open and they were very alert. At the exit, the mothers from the previous day formed a long line, and when it was her turn each received her child, with his respective uniform and identification card. They couldn't keep the children for more than ten years, said a voice through a loudspeaker. At that age, the company took them in and from that point on they lived in the supermarkets. The mothers took their children in their arms and called them by their number. That's where I had met him, I thought, as I gave him a tip. I recalled his mother's words when she caressed him: "Sixthousandfivehundred, my Sixthousandfivehundred." As a matter of fact, I could read on the identification card "Sixthousandfivehundred," and in his eyes I saw his hatred for me and for everyone who had a real name. I opened the car trunk, Sixthousandfivehundred arranged the bags inside, and before closing it he asked me, feigning disinterest, what my name was. "Fourhundredandtwenty," I answered and added: "But don't tell anyone." I saw him smile for an instant. At the hospital, number eighthundredandfiftythousand was being born at that very moment.

7

Señora Rodríguez cleared out Carlitos's room to make room for her mother-in-law. The poor woman could not stay in the hospital for this long a time, and Señor Rodríguez decided to bring her home, that's why she had a daughter-in-law to whom she had given that purse bought at a bargain sale in the Puerto de Liverpool department store. Señora Rodríguez was sulkily sweeping the bedroom, when the phone rang. "Really?" asked Señora Rodríguez with a smile and immediately grabbed her purse and left the house. She was wearing black, for in the morning she had said, "Just in case," and had put on a dress that had belonged to her sister-in-law, Laurita's mom, that was a little tight on her, but it wasn't right, in this crisis, to go out and buy a mourning gown. So, with the dress hugging her hips, she arrived at the funeral home. On the way there Señora Rodríguez recalled the chastity belt that her mother-in-law had given her as a wedding gift, along with a copy of *The Life of the Saints* in which she had highlighted the chapter dedicated to the virgins of the Church. She also recalled the day she asked her mother-in-law how Señor Rodríguez had been born and the woman's eyes had sparkled for a second, before she gave her a slap.

Señor Rodríguez was waiting for her in a sea of tears. Señora Rodríguez hugged him and for the first time in her life exclaimed: "Alone at last." At that point they realized that Señor Rodríguez already had the gout, he was bald and fat, and she had bad breath due to her poor digestion and wore bifocals; which she took out of her purse in order to read the Magnificat at the foot of the coffin. Inside, the mother-in-law was laughing.

In The Dream Clock

He had met Noemí at the end of a dream, of which all he remembered was a stickpin and the hour when he awoke: one in the morning. Noemí was going to tell him something when a pain brought him back to reality. He would have to go back and start again from that point. How would she be? Would she recognize him? They were at a party, Noemí was in a hurry . . . he felt a sharp pain between his fingernail and the flesh: "The fingernail," he thought, "the finger, the hand," and he saw himself squeezing a strange hand while he heard: "Good evening."

"Good evening," he repeated without letting go of the hand which was dragging him out of his vigil.

"Would you like to drink something, Miss . . . ?"

"Rocío," answered the young lady. Had he forgotten?

"Rocío," he spelled out silently trying to remember without losing his smile. "Might she be a friend of Noemí?" he asked himself, glancing around the room full of laughter, voices, faces. He didn't know how long he would be in the dream; realizing that he was dreaming, he had to take advantage of it.

"Rocío . . ." The voices, the laughter, and the faces zeroed in on him. He took a swig from a flavorless amber drink: "Do you know where Noemí is?"

His eyes begged for the truth. It was difficult to dream what one wanted, and he remembered the pain between his nail and the flesh, which would ultimately wake him up.

"Yes," Rocío responded. "I'll point her out." And she went away, steadily fading away among the voices, the laughter, and the faces. He followed her at a distance. At the far side of the room, in front of a window, Rocío stopped. Next to her, another woman, older, seemed to be looking for something. When she saw him, she was not surprised.

"Is it you? Yes, it's you," concluded the woman, lighting a cigarette.

"Only twenty minutes left," she continued. On her blouse she wore a stickpin, which drew him to her. He reached out his hand and the pin stuck between his nail and the flesh.

He woke up at one in the morning screaming: "Is it you? Is it you?" without recalling who he was.

8

Señor Rodríguez was an ex-seminarian when he met Señora Rodríguez, who back then was Señorita Osorio, daughter of Doña Trinidad Villa and Don Artemio Osorio, from two of the oldest families in the city and of recognized Christian values. Their courtship took place according to the best traditions, and lasted for a period of one year, even though the very distinguished Señorita Osorio was on the verge of becoming an old maid. The wedding was celebrated at six in the morning, by request of Señor Rodríguez's mother, who also planned the honeymoon and accompanied the newlyweds so that they would not be led into temptation. In Acapulco they rented a room with three beds, the mother-in-law slept in the middle; it was she who enjoyed the honeymoon the most. This is why Susanita and Carlitos met their parents much too late and were in danger of never meeting them, thanks to their grandmother, who threatened her son with divine wrath if he stained his virginity. Nevertheless, Señor and Señora Rodríguez managed to find a way. Although each had his and her own bedroom, they escaped at night and made love in the bathroom, on the stairs, or in the kitchen, where Señor Rodríguez used every means within his reach to seduce his wife. Once he shaved her downy hairs with his electric razor; another time they went rolling down the stairs together without separating, and, one other time, he covered Señora Rodríguez's body with honey in order to sweeten their union. Señora Rodríguez remembered all of this while wiping away a tear with the little handkerchief from Brussels that her Aunt Clotilde had given her and which she had in her purse the day of her mother-in-law's death.

Last Night at Night

It had to be last night, with the burning heat that we had . . .

"Open that door."

"It's open, Don Lalo."

. . . and the flies buzzing around in my head.

Between the boxes stacked against the door one could see a crack, where with a little effort a hand could fit in to turn the doorknob. The words, all the words, piled up in my head:

"They didn't find the doctor, Don Lalo, what shall I do?"

"Take down those boxes, this is suffocating."

"Doña Trini is complaining a lot, she asks for water, what shall I do?"

"Put them over here on this side, can't you see that they're blocking the way?"

"It seems that she wants you, but one cannot make out what she's saying, what shall I do?"

"What a bother, how many boxes are there?"

I believe I began placing them there a year ago, so that the kids' shouting wouldn't come through. Through the storage room one could reach the patio of the house of the deceased Arnoldo, my former landlord. Trini, his widow, was left behind with three children. They screamed like the damned when they were bathed in the patio water tank.

"Put some of the boxes there, yes there."

(Because Trini also bathed with them, and her wet slip stuck to her legs, revealing the dark triangle of her pubic hair.)

Don Arnoldo had never tried to block off the door:

"There's trust on both sides, isn't that right?"

"Of course, Don Arnoldo."

Through the cracks one could see Trinidad's breasts when she nursed Arnoldito. Damn kid, he was two and he still seemed like a tadpole; and the damned boxes allowed you to see it all.

"Stack the boxes up higher, some on top of the others."

By the time Arnoldo had been dead for three months I already knew by heart how many bricks there were in the patio, where dawn ended, and how many freckles Trinidad had on each arm.

"Send Doña Trini the rent, and she says that next month it will cost you more."

(Shit . . . this is the last straw. I can't stand it when women become bosses, and I like it even less when they're alone.)

Back then we didn't have the burning heat that we have now. The patio, recently scrubbed, would exude coolness when Trinidad, after putting the kids to sleep, would begin to sew.

"I've come to see if we can negotiate." Trinidad stuck the needle into the patched-up pants and faced me. "Don Arnoldo promised not to raise my rent, and he was a man of his word."

"He's no longer here to keep his word."

"But I am."

Trinidad went over to the water tank. . . .

"You'll have to look for another place."

The water splashed all over me. . . .

"Is that your final word?"

Her dress was getting wet. . . .

"That's it," she responded, now in my arms. I knew her body through the cracks. That body couldn't be indifferent, it had to feel the same warmth that I felt, and at that moment it was trembling, defenseless before me. She knew how to respond, there was no doubt, but we weren't even finished when she made me promise that it wouldn't happen again:

"I'm a decent woman, Medardo, if you're a real man, don't come back."

"Stack up more boxes, all the way to the top, all that you can find, do you understand?"

They stacked them up by day, and I took them down by night: from the storage room to the patio, from the patio to the corridor, the kitchen door, the kids' door, and right after. . . .

"I'm telling you that we'll be ruined."

"That's because you want it that way. I'm offering to marry you."

"What would people say?"

"What they're saying now, you think they don't know what's going on?"

"Don't be so crass, Medardo, you make me feel like a nobody."

"You aren't a nobody, you know that."

"It's because I promised Arnoldo. . . ."

"Bring more boxes, heavier ones, dammit, what do you mean, you aren't strong enough?" (I can move them all by myself and put them back every night.)

From the storage room to the patio, from the patio to the corridor. . . .

"Leave, Lalo, I beg you."

"Let's both leave, Trinidad. It's not right for you to dedicate your life to a dead person. . . ."

"Who is the father of my children."

"That's because you don't want me to be their father, too."

"No one can take his place."

"Put some metal bars on top of the boxes for support, I don't want some thief to come in through the back door."

"And why don't you put up a wall, Don Lalo?"

"Stupid kid, don't be giving me orders."

. . . the kitchen door, the kids' door, and . . .

"I'm pregnant, Medardo, it'll show soon."

"We'll get married tomorrow, Trini."

"I'd rather be dead than offend my children."

"The baby's yours just as much as they are, what difference is there between *his* and mine? The baby will have my name."

"Never, Medardo, never."

"You're crazy, Trinidad, you and I . . ."

"I never thought I would cheat on him, Medardo."

"He's dead, Trinidad."

"And *I* want to be dead because I can't forget him. So I can't have your child, look for another woman."

"But, Trini . . ."

"I'll have a wall built, Don Medardo, and you won't come into this house except through the front door."

"And my child? Have him and give him to me, you wouldn't dare get rid of him like an animal."

"Later I'll repent, and God will forgive me."

"It's not possible, Trinidad, I won't let you."

"Don't try it, just leave, I'm in charge of my own body."

"Do you love me, Trinidad? Do you love me? Answer me, Trinidad."

Trinidad kept backing up and disappeared into the brickwork; the walls grew up around me.

"Don't leave me, Trini," I shouted, "don't leave me."

And I kept shouting to her all night. All night. Yesterday the midwife entered and left Trini's house, leaving the front door closed.

"She seems very sick, Don Lalo."

"Then go and fetch a doctor, why are you telling me."

"I think she wants to talk to you."

(No, not that. I don't want to see her again, I don't care what's wrong with her, I don't want to go, no, no, Trini . . . !)

I barely made it in time to ask her to forgive me and to forgive her. She couldn't speak.

"Can you hear me?" I asked her, taking her hand. Her fingers did not move.

"If you love me, squeeze my hand," I pleaded.

A slight pressure grew stronger until she left the marks of her nails on my skin. Then her fingers loosened up.

"Trini, please, listen; why not until today, Trini; why, Trini, why?"

"Did you spend all night here alone, Don Lalo? I'll bring you a nice drink to make you feel better. You were so good to Doña Trini, if it hadn't been for you, there wouldn't have been anyone to comfort her in her final moments, since she didn't want anyone to find out."

"Be quiet, boy, and give me a cigarette."

"You're the boss. Look, they're bringing the coffin. Say, and what are we going to do with all the boxes that we removed?"

"Put them back up again, can't you see that it's freezing?"

9

Susanita and Carlitos seemed to have taken after their uncle (Laurita's father), who was nicknamed "Saint Mary" by everybody. At sixteen Susanita had been divorced once, and at thirteen Carlitos had gone off to see the world as a stowaway on an Italian ship. Free from them, Señora Rodríguez felt emancipated and got her second wind, without getting rid of her purse, for, although she could very well have exchanged it for another one, thanks to her mother-in-law's estate, she was no longer able to, it was part of her. In it she still carried her marriage certificate next to her children's birth certificates and her mother-in-law's death certificate, a dry rose that Señor Rodríguez had given her twenty years ago, the balloons and party favors from Susanita's party, and the bifocal glasses that she no longer used because she was wearing contact lenses.

One night Señora Rodríguez dreamed that she opened her purse, and from it she herself came out, opening her purse; and from this one another Señora Rodríguez came out, opening her purse again; and so on ad infinitum. Señor Rodríguez, on the contrary, dreams that the purse is a bottomless well where what goes in never comes out. He remembers the day Señora Rodríguez accidentally put her mother-in-law's picture inside the purse and soon after that she died. And also when by chance she put Señor Rodríguez's watch in the same purse and Señor Rodríguez lost the notion of time forever. That's why he gets up at three in the morning to bathe and goes to sleep at five in the afternoon, while Señora Rodríguez goes to the movies and out for a cup of coffee with her friends and pulls out the checkbook from her purse, caresses it and puts it back, just like she put away the keys to her house and even to the gates to heaven, so that no one can enter without her consent. Because Señora Rodríguez is not who they make her out to be, says Señor Rodríguez; and he must know better than I do, for he has lived with her in these pages ever since the story began.

Hide-and-Seek

No one noticed me that day. I remember it as if I'd been in many places at the same time: outside with my godfather, and inside when the priest said that he was going to give the last rites to my godmother, provided my godfather didn't see her again. I don't know why, but I realized that he wanted to be with her, and Aunt Micaela pretended not to know him and didn't let him come inside the house.

My godfather didn't move from the one spot the entire time. The shade of a tree began to run over him from top to bottom until it divided him in half. I'd never seen him like that, hidden right in the middle of the street, with foggy glasses, waiting, just like the people inside, but in silence, because the others began to pray and light candles before it was dark.

Later on people began arriving, and the patio filled with small groups, with shadowy figures, with muffled laughs. The women, sitting in a row, seemed to be covered with the same black skirt.

Throughout the entire night they held a wake for my godmother. Aunt Micaela led the lamentations and the rosary. I didn't know what to do, it was the first time I had been at a wake. My cousin and I went from one room to the other. In one of them I heard someone say: "She moved, she's not where we placed her." And then, "She was very brave, when they wanted to give her medicine to get rid of the pain she pleaded: 'Leave me alone, I'm going to die now.' " If only I had been allowed to let her know that my godfather was there, outside. . . .

"Pray for her soul, pray for her soul," the voices repeated louder and louder. My cousin and I went to play in the backyard where we couldn't hear the monotonous litany. We went through many doors until we got to the back. "Me first," screamed my cousin running ahead. The one that guessed where the other was hiding ran to home base and yelled: "One, two, three, you're it" and the other had to come out. I always lost and had to be the one to seek again. As I recall this, I get lost between so many doors, and no matter how hard I try I still can't find the exit, but I can't forget either. I was behind a planter, waiting for my cousin to find me when Aunt Micaela appeared: "And you, why don't you cry? You weren't sorry, were you? You're like your mother who never could forgive her."

"One, two, three, I'm it," I exclaimed.

Afterward everything was different. My godfather stayed all by himself in his old house. I liked to go into his bedroom to see a portrait that hung on the wall of my godfather, my godmother, and me; but we never visited or talked to him again. It seemed as if he had never existed.

One afternoon my godfather sent someone to get my mother; when she returned, she said nothing. I knew he was dead because my mother brought my portrait, the one he had in his bedroom. That's why I tried not to believe what Aunt Micaela said: "Your godfather didn't like you." My vision got blurry as if my eyes were full of splinters. I saw everything in a blur, probably as he did that day.

I asked my mother why my aunt had said that, for when I was little I used to go to the circus with my godfather and he'd buy me toys. "Don't pay any attention," she answered. I tried not to, but I did, and I learned to keep it all inside, just like they did.

The only time he phoned me was right before he died: “Why don’t you ever come over?” he asked, and added: “I miss you a lot.”

“One, two, three, you’re it,” I thought. It was the last time I played hide-and-seek.

10

Señora Rodríguez took a full-length mirror out of her purse, a gift from her aunt Clotilde, who had inherited it from Don Porfirio. A mirror that had belonged to the queen, Snow White's stepmother, according to Snow White's neighbor, a friend of number five of the seven dwarfs. Señora Rodríguez looked in the mirror and asked: "Mirror, mirror on the wall, who is the fairest in the Republic?" And the mirror replied: "The president's wife." Señora Rodríguez continued asking: "Who is the fairest in the United Kingdom?" The queen, the mirror replied. "And in the United States?" "Mrs. Bush." "And in Russia?" "Raisa Gorbachev." . . . Señora Rodríguez checked the mirror and found that there was a cassette tape hidden between the quicksilver and the glass. Señora Rodríguez put the mirror back in her purse as a souvenir of her assumption of political standing and now she's active in the opposition. Señor Rodríguez is apolitical because he doesn't have a purse.

The Best Night

Love is unrecognizable behind those old shoes covered with mud, behind that coffee stain on the shirt. However, seeing him and feeling wanted, is one and the same thing to Rebeca. The smell of his perspiration engulfs her, the smell of a man that works, that squeezes her with his callused hands, barely giving her time to become excited under his weight; without any caressing or preambles, almost in rage. But Felipe's walk, half sluggish and half deliberate, indicates that something is wrong at work; now he won't take her, he'll limit himself to drinking until the words pile up and come spilling out of his mouth. Maybe he'll cuss her out without any reason and then he'll cry. Although . . . the cigarette; he only smokes when he's happy, surely they gave him a raise, and he'll stay up all night, calculating all that he'll be able to buy, perhaps a dress for her, his "big-titted momma." It's your fault, she'd tell him, every time Felipe bit her until he made her bleed. But he had already dropped the cigarette, and he was now putting it out with his shoe as if he wanted to release his anger that way. And she who was planning to prepare some refried beans with tortillas fried in lard, just so that he'd come out and tell her that he had been fired from his job. What else could it be, all that was missing was for him to hit her and leave her covered with bruises, just like the time she came from her friend Chema's wake and somewhere between the where are you coming from and damned bitch, he put her out flat on the floor. From that incident Pelón was born, that's why he was the best kid in the family, since she spent all night creating him, enraged by the blows. And he was right, that's what she's there for; and she does whatever he wants, as long as it feels good.

Yes, love is unrecognizable behind that dirty window from where Rebeca peers, without being seen, with her lips lined with anguish.

11

Señora Rodríguez was born on the eleventh day of the eleventh month, in room number 11, in some hospital or other, where three years earlier Señor Rodríguez had been born. Both were held by the same nurse, Sister Angela, and they used the same crib where they cried, slept, and urinated for a few days, but they never knew it. Just as they don't know that the same nanny took care of them, first one and then the other. What they do know is that Chepa, the nanny, used to pinch them and threaten them that the devil was going to take them away because they were brats. One Sunday Señora and Señor Rodríguez played together at the park, and Señor Rodríguez pushed Señora Rodríguez down a slide. She scraped her knees and ran to her mother. However, neither he nor she knew that they'd marry twenty years later. Señor Rodríguez's mother pulled her son's ear, and Señora Rodríguez's mother bought her daughter some cotton candy, to comfort her.

When Señora Rodríguez was fifteen, she left a movie magazine on the seat of a movie theater, the same magazine that Señor Rodríguez later found. Both read it secretly, since their parents didn't like them to waste their time on foolish things. From then on Señora Rodríguez was predestined to carry the purse her mother-in-law would end up giving her, but she never knew it; on the contrary, she always believed that she was going to marry the crown prince of England, because at home she was always called "the queen."

No One Knows for Whom One Works

We early swimmers, spread out along the beach, were all focusing on the same spot: a long boat was crossing Audiencia Bay, pulling something that couldn't be distinguished from afar. When it got to shore three of the six men that were in it disembarked, and the remaining three sailed back by the same route, returning to the place where they had started. It wasn't until then that we realized there was a piling embedded in the sand, to which was tied a rope that went off under the sea. The three men who had stayed jumped up from their landing place and began giving signals to those at the far end. There was a guy next to us who had a belly that stuck out and milk-white legs and a T-shirt displaying the legend "I love Manzanillo." Further down there was a *gringa* in her fifties, with an orange bikini and flabby legs, who was purposefully staring at one of the men from the boat, the one that appeared to be the captain, who at the same time was shouting to the youngest of them, "Come on, asshole, what are you doing standing on dry sand, can't you see that you can't get a grip? Come to where it's wet." The boy, a kid about sixteen, slightly blond, became embarrassed, and with his head down he scooted to another spot. It took us a while to figure out what was going on; those men were fishermen and they had thrown a net across the bay. The buoys ran along the line of the net. After a while, we were all pulling the rope, the guy with the T-shirt, the *gringa*, and us, along with the three fishermen. Someone said that the fishing was good at that time and that the net would come out full of fish. Another one explained how grilled fish are prepared and how tasty they were when they were fresh out of the sea. Following the captain's instructions, we walked slowly toward the middle of the beach to meet up with those who were pulling on the other end of the net, including a few kids and an old man that had tagged along. The net weighed more than we had imagined. "Do you feel the fish?" asked the old man, and we all answered yes, with our hands stinging from pulling the rope. Paco and I joined forces to offset the *gringa* and the guy with the T-shirt: "That guy is not going to handle it with a T-shirt like that." "Nor the *gringa* wearing that bikini." "Move it," the captain yelled, "put some gusto into it." "What did he say?" asked the old man. "To move it and pull hard," Paco answered. "*What?*" the *gringa* repeated, with breasts swollen from pulling so hard. "*This* is really a solidarity pact, not like the government's," Paco commented. "Are you going to give us some fish, captain?" "Of course, just let me know how many you want." Paco tried to remember how ceviche is made, and the guy with the T-shirt offered to help: "You just slice some tomatoes and onion, and I'll take care of the rest, that's why I was a cook at a hotel in Acapulco." Paco told him that he was studying medicine and ended up talking about Marcela, his girlfriend, who had dumped him because . . .

The circle was gradually closing; the ones from the other side were now ten meters away from us and their laughter could be heard mixed with the fishermen's swearing: "Come on, don't just stand there." The sun reached the palm trees, and the number of curious people increased and began cheering us on. "There you go." "You're almost there." "Man, you guys couldn't even get it up if you tried." I could no longer feel my hands when I shouted to them, "Check it out, let's see if you can handle it." "Check it out?" repeated the *gringa*. It'd been almost an hour, and we had less than half the net in. "You'll see how neat the fish flop as they come out, Paco, it's hard to know where to begin." "Begin what?" asked the guy in the T-shirt. "To protest against the damned government," replied Paco, telling me in a low voice, "He's not a cook, I bet he's a bureaucrat." "The president is a great man," rebutted the guy. "Bush?" the *gringa* intervened. "I think this is screwed," said Paco, "I don't see any fish." "Hang on, you're not experienced in this, you'll see," I answered without much confidence, wiping the sweat off. Meanwhile, the *gringa* had managed to get next to the captain and whispered to him: "*Tonight?*" "Toonait," said the captain, shooting a glance of acknowledgment through her brassiere. Paco's eyes flashed at me, and he told me that we were dumb, the only ones pulling were us, for a long time the guy with the T-shirt had just been massaging the rope, "Don't you see his hands? They aren't even red." "Don't worry, when we're savoring our fish we won't give him any." "Well, it'll be the next time, pal," Paco said as he dropped the net. A few empty cans, some rubber boots, seaweed, and two toad fish, inflated, not edible, that was the whole contents. The kids took the boots, the guy with the T-shirt burst out laughing, the old man protested to the boatman, and he in turn to the captain, who answered that he was the authority there and to shut up or . . . Paco threw the fish back into the sea, and the *gringa* asked: "OK?" "OK," replied the captain, extending his hand. "How much is the dollar worth today?" I whispered to Paco.

12

Señora Rodríguez saw a purse just like hers at the supermarket. It was hanging on the shoulder of an old lady, whom Señora Rodríguez began to follow, not daring to speak to her. The old lady bought tomatoes, bananas, toilet paper, and detergent; Señora Rodríguez bought the same items and thought about the plane ticket to Europe that she had never bought. "I'll buy it today," she promised herself. The old lady leaned against the cash register and looked for her coin purse. From the purse emerged a pacifier, a chewed piece of gum, a sandalwood rosary, a dirty Kleenex, and the coin purse, in that order. Meanwhile Señora Rodríguez did the same, suddenly recalling all the alms that she had refused to give. "When I get home I'll send a check to the children's home," she promised herself once more. The old lady supported herself on her cane as she walked out into the street, and Señora Rodríguez, feeling tired, recalled that she never had made time to visit her Aunt Clotilde, who had recently died. "I'll place her picture in the living room as soon as I get home," Señora Rodríguez promised for the third time. The old lady turned right at the first corner, which was where Señora Rodríguez turned every day of each week, of each month, year after year. The old lady walked down three blocks; Señora Rodríguez followed her, even though she felt like she was suffocating, as she remembered her first boyfriend, whom she didn't marry. "As soon as I get home the first thing I'll do is to look up his number in the phone book." The old lady stopped in front of Señora Rodríguez's house, took out a key from her purse and opened the door. Señora Rodríguez ran, but she couldn't get there before the door locked. Señora Rodríguez knocked, shouted, rang the doorbell, without an answer and, despite all her searching she could not find the key to her house.

Blue in the Family

It's better not to mention it, Dad had said to Inés. Clara didn't understand, nor did she notice the decision in her father's look that rainy August afternoon. The same look that Inés had picked up and tucked away inside her own look. And there it was, stuck stubbornly in her memory: her father's blue pupils became watery before denouncing her. The smell of roasting corn cobs followed the rain, and this smell was followed by the smell of Jamaica fruit punch, and later the smell of bread pudding. With the smell of fresh-cut flowers Enriquito was born. Clara had seen the swelling of her sister Inés and the birth, without any explanations of the child, just as one sees the sunrise. No one asked themselves why. Inés continued with her life and the boy with his big blind eyes, quietly became part of her. No one asked themselves why he was blind either; it just had to be that way.

It's better not to mention it, father said again the day he became ill. The mother had lost her sanity some time ago. Perhaps when her only male child died, or when Enriquito was born, with blue pupils so like his grandfather's. And the mother wandered through the house without anyone noticing her, looking for her son down the halls and up the stairs, certain that he would come up at any moment. And she'd prepare cakes for him, while the father was dying.

Inés closed his eyelids and sat next to him, as he himself would have done, without any emotion. She gazed at him, and then saw her mother, looking like a butterfly dazzled by the light, walking in all directions; then she saw Enriquito, who did not see her, holding the hand of Clara, the twenty-year-old girl who hid her mongolism behind a smile. Esther felt the impulse to shout rising up in her throat, but not even a whimper came from her lips. Father was right, she said, closing her own eyes in turn.

Carlitos searched through his mother's purse when she wasn't watching and found the eyeglasses, the dry rose, Susanita's gum, and the recipe for bread pudding. He continued searching and found the first baby tooth he lost, five years before, a lock of Susanita's hair, some safety pins, and the Mexican constitution, with a few amendments made by his mother. Further down he found Aunt Clotilde's photo, one of Grandfather's tie pins (Carlitos's grandfather, not the aunt's), some earrings that had belonged to Great-grandmother (the aunt's great-grandmother, not Carlitos's), and the gun of Pancho Villa, who was Aunt Clotilde's uncle. Then he stumbled upon Maximilian's shield, Carlota's crinolines (Carlota Pérez, not the Hapsburg Carlota), Juárez's frock coat, the Declaration of Independence (the original), and Don Miguel's cassock. Later came the crown that had belonged to Charles V, Columbus's stockings, a feather from Moctezuma's crest, and a calendar, Aztec in origin. Before his wrist got stuck, with his fingers in the void, he was able to take out a mammoth's tusk, a dinosaur's tail, and a few ashes. Señora Rodríguez stopped Carlitos when he was about to pawn the purse at the Monte de Piedad, for the sum total of one thousand pesos.

German Dolls

If you look at it carefully, the bald doll is the prettiest one of all, with her round cranium and her blackish eyes. I don't remember if her wig was blond or brunette; it wasn't black; there are hardly any dolls with black hair, they have to be blonds, brunettes, or redheads, and have blue eyes. I had a lot like that. My dark hands held them with fear of getting them dirty, and I cooed to them for a while before sending them to the concentration camp, where I undressed them, bathed them with icy water, and shaved their heads, as I saw it done to the Jews in a movie on TV. Except that my blond dolls with blue eyes were German not Jewish. They say that's what Germans look like; I never met any. At school the majority of us were dark, some more than others, but not white white. We made fun of the only blond kid, whom we called Cócono due to his freckles, because his mother was dark and everyone asked her where did she get Cócono, so blond. After hearing the same things over and over again, she became annoyed and took him out of school. That's why my dolls had to be German, even though in reality they were *gringas,* because my uncle brought them to me from across the border, but I didn't know if the *gringos* didn't like Jews either, so I continued pretending that they were German and I was Jewish and I couldn't keep them. I found names like Helga, Gretel and Marlene, to baptize them so that they could go to heaven after I burned them, for they say that the children who die without being baptized go to Limbo and cry when someone spills salt. They stank real bad when they were crackling, and soon they ended up twisted, scorched, and melted. When I turned twelve I was given María. When I pressed her stomach she said ma-ma. From the first time I heard her I knew that I wasn't going to do to her what I had done to the others, and that's why I named her María and hid her, so that no one would make fun of me, like they did Cócono's mother, asking where did she come from, so white with me so dark. But even though she was hidden, I feared that someone would find her and mock me. Her blue eyes watched me in fear when I approached her with the hot burning stick. I didn't stop crying until her eyes turned blackish and then I put a bandage over them. "It's for your own good, María," I explained, smearing her with soot from the same half-burned stick so that she didn't look so white. Finally I pulled off her wig, and I laid her on my bed. Now no one will believe that María is not Mexican, or Jewish.

Señora Rodríguez decided to clean out her purse to start the day off right. She opened it as if it were the first time, and with the same devotion with which she had inserted each object, once again she began taking them out one by one. The first thing that appeared was a couple of size five insoles. Señora Rodríguez threw them in the trash, while at the same time removing her shoes and tossing them into a corner. At that minute her mother-in-law was completely erased from her mind. In stocking feet, Señora Rodríguez removed from her purse a postcard from Acapulco, sent by her niece Laurita; and she took off her sweater because she was hot. Never again did Señora Rodríguez think about Laurita, or her sister-in-law, or her brother. Señora Rodríguez took off her blouse and slacks, after having removed from the purse Carlitos's pacifier, Susanita's fancy shoes, the dress she wore on her fifteenth birthday, and the phone bill from February 1965; whereupon Señora Rodríguez completely forgot about Carlitos, Susanita, and everything that had occurred before 1965. At the moment that Señora Rodríguez tossed out her marriage certificate, she removed her wedding band, and, incidentally, all memory of Señor Rodríguez. After emptying the purse of all its contents, Señora Rodríguez looked in the mirror and didn't recognize herself. Señor Rodríguez found her naked, crawling around the living room, dragging the purse, whose contents were spread throughout the house. Señor Rodríguez figured out what had happened and rushed to put everything back into the purse before it was too late. In his haste he mixed up days with nights, present with past, and joined an Ash Wednesday with a Good Friday. When he finished closing the purse he looked at his watch: it was seven o'clock in the morning on the nineteenth day of September, 1985. Señora Rodríguez recovered her memory in the middle of an earthquake that measured eight on the Richter scale. Inside the purse, chaos prevailed.

Between the Lines

I am the aunt. In any respectable story an aunt is indispensable; she may be the bad one, the rich one, the old maid, or the go-between, and I'm no exception. I have a mustache, I wear black, and I'm single, I see it all, I hear it all, and without me América, Agamenón, and Rosendo couldn't live. They're my cats, of course, and they tip-toe through the text or hide under the bed, where Julio and Laura don't make love, or they stay behind a door and listen . . . : "Aunt?" I stroke my mustache and rub my hands before answering: "Yes?" The scream comes from Laura's imagination, who doesn't dare confess the anguish that makes her look into the mirror time after time; finally she tells me: "Aunt, do you think I'm attractive?" Sitting in a corner of the story, I see Agamenón pass slowly by, very slowly, with his tail in the air. Laura is forty and has the attractiveness of a woman who feels wanted; only an idiot like Julio, her husband, doesn't see that. Now I see América and Rosendo pass by, I could swear that they are laughing, and I can almost guess at whom. Laura, with her eyes fixed on the mirror, holds her breath and sticks out her chest, smiles. It has been a long time since I saw her like this, pensive, unreachable. . . . Agamenón from the edge of the page looks at me out of the corner of his eye; he wants to jump to the next one, to get ahead of the narration. "Agamenón? Agamenón? Wait, Agamenón." Two pages further ahead I find him snooping around another character. He looks as if he came out of a fairy tale, but the truth is that I've known him for some time, since Laura was a child. He is the perfect lover, twenty years of loving her in spite of his own wife, and Julio. Laura comes running from the previous page: "Aunt, how did you find out?" I feign indifference while I knit a scarf for Rosendo. América is pregnant, and I don't know from which of the two, but this is material for another story. Laura sees Ricardo, openly stares at his face, she stops at the mouth that speaks her language, then the eyes which invest her with womanhood, which remind her of Julio, blind Julio. . . . "Aunt, it's not my fault that Ricardo continues to love me, right?" América comes by shamelessly with her enlarged stomach. I realize that something has happened, something that wasn't written. Ricardo approaches, his anxiety is reflected in Agamenón's pupils: "I shouldn't be in this story, Aunt, if we could only retell it, without Julio. . . ." I clear my throat, yank off the scarf, and begin again. Rosendo can wait.

15

Aunt Clotilde, Don Porfirio's lover, in spite of the fact that she was Pancho Villa's cousin, was Señora Rodríguez's favorite character in her younger days. Señora Rodríguez knew her aunt by hearsay, because, when she was born, Aunt Clotilde had already made history in Europe. Aunt Clotilde had no children. From far away she became fond of her niece and began writing to her without the permission of the girl's parents, who considered her the black sheep of the family. Señora Rodríguez clandestinely read the letters her aunt sent from Europe, and dreamed of Paris, *la belle époque, art nouveau,* Mata Hari, and Aunt Clotilde dressed like a princess. In turn, Aunt Clotilde imagined that her niece continued to be a little angel.

Aunt Clotilde was on the *Ipiranga* when Don Porfirio left for France. Contrary to popular belief, the true reason for his trip was the accusation that Clotilde's father had made that Don Porfirio had seduced his daughter, who was still a minor. Upon Don Porfirio's death, Aunt Clotilde traveled across Europe, and didn't return to Mexico until fifteen years after the end of World War II. When she arrived she was disappointed to see her niece tied up to that horrible purse and said only, "I brought you a hankie from Brussels." Señora Rodríguez thanked her and put it in her purse, next to *The True History of Both World Wars,* written by Aunt Clotilde, where she revealed that the heads of the warring nations fell in love with her and declared war because of her; for the aunt never denied that she was frivolous and granted her favors equally to one and all. Only her sense of humanity made her return to Mexico, saving the world from World War III (pages 5,000 to 7,000 in the previously mentioned book, which is inside Señora Rodríguez's purse).

With Respect to the Sky

A display of birds broke the afternoon silence. Lined up on the electrical power wire, some on their feet and others on their heads, they interwove their songs, forming a net that settled on the cluster of houses. The man who was entering the town at that moment felt this tumult of voices weaving a net around him. As he moved forward down the main street, bordered by the curiosity of its inhabitants, hidden behind windows, the melodious net cast itself over the pavement, its mesh growing more and more defined. The visitor began to walk bent over, as if to avoid stepping on the pattern.

It was Good Friday. The population, after easing its conscience in the confessional booth, was waiting for Holy Saturday in order to sin again. Some, however, didn't resist the temptation of lying, coveting their neighbor's wife, or fornicating in silence, in the face of the increasingly stooped-over walk of the stranger, on whom they cast their regrets, their trespasses, their animosity. The traveler wasn't able to avoid them, as he was trapped in the warbling grid that surrounded him.

His first fall was due to a slander that got wrapped around his feet. Then he slipped on a poorly hidden adultery. He tried to scream before falling again, but the deafening noise of the birds prevented him. Flat on the ground, with his face stuck to the asphalt, he felt hot air burning his lungs.

The next day the sky was clean. No one knew at what time the birds had migrated. The municipal street cleaners picked up the net, full of waste from the previous night. The body of the stranger was buried in a pauper's grave. Only the apprentice who took him to the amphitheater noticed the incipient wings that were hidden under his shirt.

16

Señora Rodríguez's gynecologist discovered that she has a baby tooth, not under her pillow, nor as a souvenir, but in Señora Rodríguez's own gums. And, to top it off, it's loose, which demolishes all her experience, her maturity, her liberalism, and her sex appeal. She who has always believed she was seductive, and now all it took was for her to open her mouth to prove the contrary. "It's a dirty trick of destiny," Señora Rodríguez sniffles while taking a rattle, for which she has special predilection ever since she found out about the tooth, out of her purse. "How will I look with a missing tooth? It will surely fall out while I'm making love, and I don't doubt that I will swallow it and it'll get caught in my throat. How the paramedics are going to laugh at me if they find me suffocated in those circumstances. The worst of it is that, if they suspect homicide, my husband will end up in jail naked, and there someone will . . . The best thing to do is write my will and observe abstinence until it falls out. And the pain of the gums when a tooth is going to come in can even cause fever and diarrhea. I remember that my mother used to rub our gums with cognac to numb them. And what if it comes in crooked? Me at this age with braces; so what, as long as it's okay. Had I known, instead of going to the gynecologist I would have gone to the dentist and perhaps he would have told me that I was pregnant again," Señora Rodríguez sighs, taking a sip of calcium supplement, just in case.

Without Knowing That It Is You

The afternoon begins with a new denial, a quick glance at the mirror confirms it: no, you're not there, you can't be that bleached blond who wears dark glasses; slamming the door, you go out to look for yourself, your hair flying behind you. Among guffaws and clinking wine glasses, someone behind the door says, "Where is she gong?" "Let her be, you know how she is," your ex-husband answers. "It probably bothered her to see me with Ofelia, too bad, it's her problem, she'll be back in a while, you'll see." At the same time Ofelia is flirting with your partner and he with her, just like the other times, but this time, you are no longer here.

The street greets you full of noise and sunshine, clearing your mind of the cigarette smoke, but you continue to feel lost. Ofelia and your ex-husband no longer interest you, only you matter, like twenty years ago, when you hid deep inside yourself for the first time to escape from suspicious looks. Since that day you're a stranger in your own body: you peer through your eyes, you don't recognize yourself, and you run away from that other without knowing that it is you. The last thing you remember about yourself is that your mother prohibited you from inviting friends home because of that business about your father. "You don't have to tell anyone," she ordered, and you understood that she was giving you permission to lie. Later you learned to invent excuses, to pretend, to deny yourself. . . . If only you could go far away, where no one knows you, before you completely forget the dark girl that you abandoned somewhere twenty years ago. Perhaps there's still time to save her from that senseless life, except where did you leave her? Which way can you go? The sun makes the sidewalk sparkle, your ankles hesitate between continuing on or turning left. You choose the latter, guided by the murmur that whirls in the air and vanishes in the heights. You look up, seeking open windows, peering faces, and your look is stifled in the midst of the buildings, which rise above awnings and bars. No, you can't be there either, behind those broken windows where hope is fading. You turn dubiously, and take the only taxi that comes by. Your overworked high heels haven't yet gotten used to your swollen feet. The taxi stops in front of a park at the outskirts of the city. You get out and sit down under the shade of a tree, you look like an indecisive shadow. "I can't return," you tell yourself, you don't want to continue acting out the same role of the frivolous, independent femme fatale. But you know that you don't have anywhere to go, you'd have to break all the mirrors in order to start over again, and you don't dare. You're afraid of finding nothing behind those glasses, behind that blond hair. You prefer to continue pretending, crouched inside yourself, waiting for someone to rescue you. You'll say that you went out to buy some cigarettes, you'll ask for a drink, you'll give a kiss to . . . anyone at all, and you won't put up with the sarcastic laughter.

Little by little, thoughts are yielding to sensations: it smells like a pine tree, it's hot, you're thirsty, very thirsty. The fatigue wraps around your arms, closes your eyes, you begin to fall asleep. Fake smiles, half truths, an unfinished letter, are mixed up in your unconscious; had you finished that letter addressed to your mother, you'd know who you are, but you were afraid to face the truth. You've always been a coward and a sham. As a child you were the perfect image of order and responsibility, in order to please the adults and not be compared with anyone. You knew that you weren't like the rest of the girls, who had a mama and a papa.

Your father spent all his life going on one trip after another; you didn't know him; finally, your mother explained, in her own way, that he didn't exist. So you made up an ideal one, with the eyes of one artist, the smile of another, the voice of . . . and when you were asked about him you became confused and he ended up looking just like any papa: loving, strict sometimes, and so busy that he was never home. You scrupulously kept the secret day after day, anticipating the suspicious question with: "Today we received a letter from Dad." Or signing report cards with a fictitious name and even calling him on the phone in front of others. On Father's Day you were the most enthusiastic in making a gift only to end up hiding it in the closet next to the one from the previous year, and the one before that, and . . . you couldn't go on like that, that's why when he "died in an accident outside the country," you cried in front of your classmates and believed that your reputation was safe, but they all knew. No one had ever believed your story. You had to get out of school and dye your hair blond in order to fool yourself. But, you spent hours in front of the mirror, envisioning male features through your own. You didn't look like your mother, so you had to look like him. You began to see him here and there. One day he was a literature professor; another, a cab driver or a banker. They all had your face and mocked your anxiety, your animosity, your insolence, until from so much seeing yourself in the faces of others, you forgot your own. Although, perhaps he knows you and is waiting for the precise moment to approach you, or perhaps he already did it and you didn't know. It's not easy to ask a stranger, "Are you my daughter?" What would you tell him? How would he react? And, what if nothing happened? You can't escape so many questions, wherever you go your father continues to follow you, intervening in your life: "You are the daughter of an unknown father." "Your mother is a whore." "You are worth nothing, you are worth nothing, you are worth nothing." That's why you married the first man who asked you. You would have a last name, perhaps you'd eventually love him. Love? Soon you became aware of your frigidity. Your father was there, between the two of you. Your husband began to drink, to seek consolation, while you continued to run, further away each time, looking for love in Luis's arms, in Hector's, in Alberto's. No one can live without love, except that you are incapable of loving any man because you aren't capable of loving yourself. Your own insecurity shames you, it makes you hate yourself. That's why you don't want to wake up, you're better off that way, in the darkness that surrounds you. You don't realize that you begin to laugh and sing because you dream that you're almost happy, no one can expose you there. You tremble, your body shudders a bit, and then it begins relaxing until it remains still. A sudden ladder takes you out of the semidarkness of your night. You ascend and you see, from above, a woman lying under a tree, with painless shoes, her blond hair spread out on the grass, dark glasses in one hand and a broken mirror in the other. You don't recognize her. While you continue to climb higher and higher, in another part of the city the wine glasses also are empty.

17

Calling Elisa made her feel terribly lethargic, thought Señora Rodríguez while searching for her address book in her purse. She would have to wish her a happy new year, explain to her that she wanted to call her earlier and hadn't been able to, something entirely false but necessary if she wanted to continue with the true purpose of her call: to find out if she would collaborate in the rest homes. So she had no alternative. But perhaps, she would first call Carlota, Señora Rodríguez told herself, not finding her address book, which, even though it was also bothersome, at least it would be more spontaneous to begin a conversation with her, that is if she wasn't busy and didn't ask her to call back later on. On second thought, Señora Rodríguez contradicted herself, as she extracted from her purse the first volume of *The True Story of Both World Wars,* she preferred to call Victoria. Would she remember her after so many years? She couldn't stand the thought of asking, "Do you remember me?" It was probable that she would answer yes; however, it was possible that she wouldn't, which would leave Señora Rodríguez, obviously, without a topic of discussion. And Marcela? Her phone is always busy, sighed Señora Rodríguez, terminating her search. Don't even consider Leticia, decided Señora Rodríguez, closing her purse abruptly, one never knows if one will catch her at a bad time. "They're a bunch of neurotics," she proclaimed and unplugged the phone so that no one would bother her.

Office Machine

A day to me is the sum of twenty-four hours, one thousand four hundred and forty minutes, and eighty-six thousand four hundred seconds ticked off one by one, even though you can try to convince me of the contrary with that "nothing-happened face" when you get off the train after enjoying a week of vacation with your wife and your rosy-cheeked children. Everything is in order, right, Lupita? you proclaim so very calmly that you resemble a town church bell calling everyone to the rosary, sooo innocent, sooo certain about me: you call and I come to you, a punctual woman-clock who arranges her time to meet your time.

"I need an efficient secretary, salary commensurate with abilities," read the newspaper ad. My abilities were nonexistent, but you made sure I knew what you needed me to know: flowers for Claudia's birthday, reservations for the wedding anniversary, trips, theater functions, everything went through my hands before it went through your wife's, even your children. First it was for an hour or two, then the entire afternoon, with your permission or without it, and I took care of them because they were yours, because of those eyes of theirs so full of you that they seemed to kiss, just with a look. And you were so proud of them and of your wife who took very good care of them, who didn't neglect them, who . . .

She always arrived ten minutes before you, and please don't tell him anything, Lupita, he doesn't need to know. And me, no, it's not worth it, he's very tired, but fearing that someday you would find out and they would no longer be brought to me and I who had grown accustomed to them and they to me. I had never seen any twins so alike and who had learned to lie so quickly. At five they already knew how to say that they had spent the afternoon playing with Mom at the park instead of with me. Whenever you left for a trip, the office overflowed with laughter and games that you almost discovered, more than once: "Señor Ochoa's contract, Lupita, Lupita, *please* what's wrong, why are you so distracted? Why is there candy in the files, Lupita?" And those colored prints, I couldn't explain how they ended up in the price lists. In any case, the business functioned in spite of my "extravagances," your trips and your children: "Lupita, take care of the boys." I saw less and less of your wife. The boys arrived with the maid or alone because Mom was still changing into the dresses I selected in your name. Your children began to comment about how nice "Uncle Héctor" was to them. He took them to the movies, bought them chocolates, and all he asked was that they didn't tell Dad, so that they wouldn't be scolded for eating between meals or for taking time away from their homework since Dad was very strict about that, even though there was nothing wrong with it, that's why Uncle Héctor gave them those small pleasures, and in return, of course, they should let him be with Mom who was so lonely, the poor woman, because Dad was always busy or on a trip, and that's how we went about falsifying your life more and more without your knowing it. I used to see you arrive with gifts for Claudia and the children, and for me the paperweight with a pen and the same question as always: "Is everything fine, Lupita?" And I nodded my head trying to excuse Claudia's excessive expenditures, everything is so expensive, especially when one has a plaything like Héctor, so young, so well dressed, so like a bell that he rings in Claudia's ears and on Claudia's skin. And you near bankruptcy in spite of your effort, in spite of mine: "We cannot reduce my family's expenditures, that doesn't have anything to do with the business, Lupita; by the way, tomorrow I'll be leaving for vacation with Claudia and the children, please take care of everything and when I return . . ." Héctor will be waiting with eager lips, and the kids will play with him, Claudia will play with you, you will play like you don't realize that she and that I . . .

18

Señora Rodríguez took out the phone directory from her purse, opened it from the back, and pointed her finger at random; then she looked down at the place where her finger was pointing and read: Valle Inclán, Ramón. "Valle Inclán," it sounds familiar, said Señora Rodríguez as she dialed the phone number that appeared next to the name. On the other end of the line someone answered: "Yes?"

"Is Mr. Del Valle home?" asked Señora Rodríguez.

"He's busy," replied the voice. "Who's calling?"

Señora Rodríguez hesitated and finally gave her name.

"One moment please," the voice requested. Two minutes later Señora Rodríguez heard: "Yes?" to which she inquired with: "Are you Mr. Del Valle?"

"At your service, Señora Rodríguez."

"Oh, do you know me?" she replied in a soprano voice.

"Of course," he continued, "naturally, how were you able to reach me?"

"I saw your number in the directory."

"I didn't know that there were such specialized directories, where did you obtain it?"

"Let me look." Señora Rodríguez took out the book from her purse again. "Well, let's see," began Señora Rodríguez, "it's the . . ." and here she interrupted herself; the cover read "Dictionary," not "Directory." She looked once more under Valle, and when she got to Valle Inclán, Ramón, she found the numbers that she had dialed: 1866–1936. When Señora Rodríguez picked up the receiver again, it was giving the classic busy signal.

Geography Lesson

Barberena, Gloria?"

"Here, professor."

Barberena, with her slender and firm waist underneath the plaid uniform, stands up and begins to brandish her words with affectation and boldness.

"Africa is located in . . ."

And without hesitating she begins to invent what she doesn't know, taking full advantage of her choir-girl smile, unaware, perhaps, of the effect she provokes in me. From my desk, where I'm exposed to the scrutinizing look of fifty pairs of eyes, I make an effort to distract myself by constructing in my mind the puzzle that is Gloria Barberena, starting from that mouth that tries to persuade me of her knowledge, from those eyes that look inward, as if they were reading in her mind the geography lesson, from that straight flowing hair that falls down her neck to the seam of her blouse, where the trail is completely lost: the austere plaid uniform, reminiscence of the chastity belt, dams up my imagination, which is about to overflow my thick glasses. With my index finger I run through Level IIIC roster, to find Barberena; she's the fourth one on the list, after Ahumada, Ascencio, and Banda. Yes, here she is, Barberena, with her chest thrust forward, in spite of that horrible fabric. . . . "Africa is located in . . ." Africa's borders are less remote than her waist, which I would place halfway between the seam of her skirt and her head, now lightly inclined, no doubt, upon the limits of the dark continent. Limits that extend far beyond what's reasonable, I suspect, focusing on the uniform, trying to situate the diminutive nipples, the tender pubic fuzz, the bellybutton, over that plaid grid and without other references but a piece of leg covered by a thick stocking, small hands that sprout from narrow cuffs, and the dark skin which I suppose extends underneath the merciless uniform without finding the exit. Africa's climate, in Gloria's voice, makes me sweat: I've just discovered the exact location of the groin thanks to an imperceptible knee movement, which caused a crease where I let my glance slide while I slide my fingers over . . . the grade book, and I write down a ten for number four, who, gratefully, sits down and carelessly crosses her legs, revealing her thigh. "She will go far," I tell myself, writing down a point in my favor while I ask: "Cásares, Adriana?" Before I can focus on her, she replies:

"Here, professor," directing her eyes to the bottom of my pants from where they slowly ascend, very slowly. It's a sure bet that my socks don't match my suit, I think, hoping that her gaze doesn't linger too long on the coffee stains that I wasn't able to remove this morning and on the torn pocket. Trying not to be noticed I pull my jacket down to the most convenient height to avoid a deliberate inspection of my crotch. I try not to move, and I suck in my stomach as much as possible when I feel that a button is about to pop off. The knot of my tie is choking me and heat is rushing to my face, along with Adriana's eyes which meet up with mine, tired and blinking. The little plaid squares are beginning to dance, and I'm only on number five.

19

Susanita and Carlitos were prepared for their First Communion by their grandmother. The good lady was determined to implant in her grandchildren the eternal truths and good customs that she had always practiced, along with endless prayers that they had to recite before getting up, going to bed, eating, and even before bathing; this they did with their clothes on, due to fear of falling into temptation. And so that the children wouldn't forget her teachings, she had some cards printed with an illustration of the Virgin and the following text: "Remembrance of Susanita and Carlitos Rodríguez's First Communion, celebrated on May 10, 1965." One of the cards lies at the bottom of Señora Rodríguez's purse. No matter how often she took it out with the purpose of proving her children's innocence, she wasn't able to convince Susanita's ex-husband that she hadn't cheated on him with the caretaker of the zoo's tiger exhibit; nor the police that Carlitos wasn't capable of smoking marijuana on an empty stomach. "And to think that my mother-in-law had ten thousand cards printed just in case," sighed Señora Rodríguez, crossing herself and smacking a kiss on her thumb while she recalled the thousands of novenas and fervent prayers offered by her mother-in-law to guarantee her own entrance in heaven, before the church decided that there would no longer be plenary indulgences.

The Congregation in the Park

To Cecilia Eudave

I began to go to the park out of boredom. I would arrive and sit on the first bench to the right. At first I used to spend the afternoon all alone, reading, and sometimes staring between the lines without paying attention to whatever I was looking at. A few afternoons had passed when a man sat down next to me and also began to read. He was wearing a blue suit. Suddenly he looked at me, smiling with complicity, showing me his book, which was the same as mine.

"Do you like García Márquez?" he asked me.

I didn't want to disappoint him and I answered yes, even though I was just beginning to read the book.

He's my favorite author, he continued with the familiarity one gets when something is shared. I'm glad; these days it's difficult to find someone who reads, I remarked, concluding the conversation. Will you come tomorrow? he said by way of farewell. I don't know, I answered as I left. I didn't think about this encounter until the next day on my way to the park. The weather was pleasant and I had finished my chores ahead of time, so I could take a few hours to relax, I told myself, without anyone asking me about it. When I arrived I saw the bench was empty and felt at ease; I didn't intend to renew yesterday's chat. I was there to take advantage of the last summer days. I didn't notice her presence until I got up to leave. The first thing that I saw was a book, my book, that is to say, her book. A woman was looking at me over the top of her glasses, waiting for me to look up. Are you the person who's studying García Márquez? Yes, I answered. We also admire him. Who's "we"? I asked feeling annoyed. All of us, she said. "All?" Yes, we who de-vo-ur García Márquez, of course. Perhaps you know them? I don't, but he does, she explained showing me a picture of the man with the blue suit; it was he who asked me to come, he wasn't able to come today, perhaps tomorrow; she finished speaking, giving me her hand. I ended up laughing about the whole incident; they had played an innocent prank on me, I thought.

I stopped going to the park for three days because I was busy with other matters, but on the fourth day, I decided to go again. I attributed my restlessness to work and to being tired, and I needed some fresh air. When I got to the bench I saw them. They seemed to have been waiting for me for a long time. I greeted them, obligated by the anxious looks they fixed on my face. Have you bought Gabo's latest book? they exclaimed all at once, making room so that I could sit among them. In spite of our uncomfortable position, the afternoon went by quickly between commentaries about the pages each one had read. Around seven, one of them pushed forward to say, Tell us something about García Márquez's life, you must know some interesting details. For the second time I didn't want to disappoint them, and I began telling the little I knew. From that day on I began to go every day, even during winter. Now there were more than one hundred of us who gathered around the bench. The password was: Do you read Gabo? and, even if they didn't, no one dared confess it. I was in the middle of all of them discoursing on *One Hundred Years of Solitude,* when I saw the man in the blue suit approaching. He sat down on the bench to the left with a book in his hands. My followers fell silent. We looked at each other in suspense. I was the first one to break it. García Márquez? I asked pointing to the book. And rubbing his chin with his fingers, he answered: No, Fernando del Paso. The others heard us without knowing what to do; then they began to get up one by one and walk in all directions and bump into each other. And they were still bumping into each other when I left them.

Aunt Clotilde is sad; she found in her niece's purse a pamphlet from 1910, bearing the slogan "True Suffrage, No Reelection." Immediately she recalled Juventino Rosas's waltzes, Angela Peralta's arias, the popular songs and the afternoon parties of her youth. When Señora Rodríguez's father didn't know Señora Rodríguez's mother, he did know her, Aunt Clotilde, who wasn't an aunt yet and who had cute dimples on her cheeks and others even cuter on the back of her knees and . . . who might have been Señora Rodríguez's mother if it hadn't been for Don Porfirio who, while passing down the Alameda one afternoon, stopped his carriage in front of Aunt Clotilde, whose figure revealed itself through her silk dress. That's destiny, thought Don Porfirio when he saw her. In fact the president's destiny was so long that it got entangled with hers. The horses ran wild, and Don Porfirio, without destiny, would have died had Aunt Clotilde not cast to him one end of her own destiny.

In that entanglement the elections got confused with the slender waist of the aunt; the constitution with her French umbrella; and Don Francisco y Madero with her tiny pigskin boots. Don Porfirio went after Aunt Clotilde following his destiny, and, when Limantour tried to stop him, destiny broke in two. The best half was kept by Aunt Clotilde, as proved in *The Other Side of the Mexican Revolution,* volume 95, written by the aunt and published by the Joaquín Mortiz publishing house.

No-Man's-Land

We were a family just like every family, with a house just like other houses, until he arrived.

We took him in when she had been living with us for two years, a seniority that gave her the right to use the house as she fancied. It was all the same to her if she slept under the stairs, on a bed, or in the garden. Perhaps that's why she became resentful when she heard him playing and making noise in front of the house and realized that in order to open the carport, we had to first close the door that led to the patio, leaving her in an intermediate zone that she didn't like because she felt trapped. She did not understand that our intention was to protect her from any possible attack. We did not know him yet. He had arrived at the house limping, and even in this state he inspired fear. I do not know if it was out of necessity or out of caprice that we became fond of him. After a few weeks he was so strong he didn't allow anyone to come near the fence.

We began parking the cars outside the carport, so that we wouldn't have to restrain him every time we wanted to take the cars out. Later, we paved the little garden adjacent to it, which he had destroyed with all his digging, and we raised the wall higher so that he wouldn't be bothered by the kids in the neighborhood. Finally we decided to build the wall all the way across and remove the gate, having noticed that he had learned to open it. We ended up isolated from the street. Luckily, there was a back door, which, even though we had to go around, became the only alternative to getting rid of him.

We did not realize that she had observed our movements during that period and that this side of the house was all she had left. From the stairs, with her round eyes she would watch the comings and goings of every family member. At first we did not notice, but day after day her look became more insistent, especially if she heard his noises when he scratched himself, when he drank water, or when he chased after a bird.

The first one to become intimidated was Raulito. Can you come with me to the kitchen, Mama? he asked me one evening, and when we passed by her, he made a detour. I told Raúl about it. It's absurd, he answered, it's all in your imagination, I do not want the boy to become a good-for-nothing. I said nothing about it after that.

The situation became worse in spite of our attempts to ignore her. And we didn't dare ask for help because it was ridiculous that we were afraid of her, so loyal, so cute, so threatening.

At eight in the evening I used to go out and feed him. I would close the door that led to the patio before opening the door to the carport, and, after closing it again, I would feed her. Today I repeated each step as always, except that when I reopened the patio door, she stopped me with a look of determination not to let me enter. My kids were away on vacation, and my husband would be home late. I realized that this was the opportunity she had been waiting for. I felt trapped when I saw her at the entryway, blocking my way. I tried to mollify her, but her hair bristled and I gave up. Now I am in the intermediate zone, waiting for someone to rescue me. From here I can see the keys to the rear door, on top of the table where my husband left them. She knows this and begins to bare her fangs.

21

As far as anything happening, nothing had happened that afternoon, except for the pictures. Señora Rodríguez closed the old photo album as if she had read the story of her life for the very first time. Her astonishment turned into nostalgia and then into a bad mood. The rest of the afternoon she wasn't able to erase from her mind those unreachable images. She tried to place yesterday's faces with those of today and something was either missing in them or something was left over. Señora Rodríguez went outside. When she got into the car she observed herself in the rearview mirror comparing her face with the one she had just put away in a drawer, with identical results. Absentmindedly, Señora Rodríguez went into the supermarket; the prices were also different; twenty years ago no one imagined that things could change so much. She couldn't concentrate on shopping, thinking about the little sunburned faces, of Susanita and Carlitos, looking at her from the photographs. I wonder where they are now? she asked herself, taking Carlitos's pacifier and Susanita's gum out of her purse. On her way back home she turned on López Cotilla and went up La Paz. She went up to the address where she used to live when she was single. She knocked with the pretext of paying a visit to the new tenant, who surely would understand the reason for her boldness. A maid opened the door: "No, the lady of the house is not home, and I cannot let you come in." Señora Rodríguez looked in from outside. Where there used to be a large window a wall stood; the living room was now a library; the fountain was now covered over; it seemed as if the house were hiding from her. She quickly said good-bye and went on her way. Señor Rodríguez was watching TV when she threw herself at him, covering him with kisses. "Hasn't anything happened?" she asked her husband. "Of course not," he responded. "What could happen?" Señora Rodríguez took his hand and replied, "You're right," while she recalled the mumps, the tantrums, the death of one of her grandmothers, the death of the other one, the devaluation, the first gray hair. . . . "You know what?" she whispered in his ear. "I still keep contraceptives in my purse." . . . Señor Rodríguez turned off the television. At the age of fifty-five, Señora Rodríguez became pregnant for the third time.

And the Crows Cawed

"At dawn take out the 'compadre' and charge him with desertion."

"Yes, captain."

Do not worry, Father, at daybreak I will have the answer. I have waited up so many nights, wanting to dream while swatting away the memories with my hand time after time, feeling them fluttering above my head: Jacinta was there, leaving a thousand times through the same door, leaving it ajar. . . . And me twisting on the bed out of pure shame. Ramón was like a brother, we were never apart; together we went to the hills to hunt quail, we learned to ride bareback, to smoke and to talk about women, in time. He always won at everything, and I admired him, even though at times I also envied him; but his sincere smile won me over, the same smile with which he won Jacinta over. He met her first and cheerfully made her his wife, never imagining that anyone, least of all me, would stab him in the back. That's why he asked me to act as godfather for his boy. He began to do very well; every day he was more prosperous, she was more and more a woman, and the kid just as brave as he and as handsome as she, no doubt about that. I was the one who remained behind, like their shadow, watching them grow. Ramón had made me his administrator. "If it weren't for you, compadre," he always said, making me feel as if I were his brother, his younger brother. The envy that I carried inside began to get to me. "What does he have that I don't have?" I told myself, looking at Jacinta, who once in a while showed a cunning that only prostitutes possess. "She doesn't steal it, she inherits it," murmured the gossips, meaning that Jacinta was illegitimate. This made things easier for me. "It'll be a game," I thought, calculating everything, except what happened. When I realized, it was too late; Jacinta was more powerful than I and knew how to get what she wanted: to dominate, to possess the will and the feelings of everyone else. "I won't be weak like my mother," she warned me each time I protested her coldness. "No man will humiliate me." She appeared to hate the world, but it was the way in which she hated that attracted me even more. I fell in love like a kid, Father. She, on the other hand, continued calling me "compadre," even when she was in my arms. "Don't make fun of me," I pleaded to her, and she silenced me by holding me tighter. And I feeling like a wretch and dying of jealousy. Jacinta continued being Ramón's wife, and I continued being the loser, because Ramón was either blind or she had him totally bewitched. "Take care of her, compadre," he used to tell me when he went out of town. And my soul was churning up within my body. I recalled our friendship, which he had never stained, and I felt like screaming, asking him to forgive me; then I recalled Jacinta, with her legs wrapped around mine, and I lacked the strength to do so. "Perhaps she loves me," I thought. If I had been certain that Jacinta loved me, I would not have deceived Ramón, I would have said it to his face, but only God knows if the one deceived wasn't me. Now Ramón is already buried. He died all of a sudden, that's what everyone believes, only I know that he was dead while he was alive. He had become an old man; it took only two years for the pretense to consume him. "Can you hear the crows cawing, compadre?" he asked me, before his wrinkles became permanent, simulating mouths that one day had been smiles. "No, Ramón," I answered, "I don't hear anything." "Can it be that you don't want to hear?" That was the last thing he said, staring at Jacinta without any reproach, without any denunciation. I remained in doubt forever. "Compadre," I used to hear him calling at me in the night, "do you hear them? They are cawing, the crows, compadre." And a chill made me grind my teeth.

Jacinta did not return again; that's when I understood her words: "I don't want to owe you anything, compadre. I swear that I'll repay you for all that you suffered for me," she told me, the last time she was with me. When we were finally free from each other, Jacinta revealed what she really was and I what I had been: a poor devil, a wretch who lost his best friend because of passion. I realized that I was all alone. No longer could I get drunk with Ramón and get into a hell of a fight or cry with him. I would have liked to confess to him that the little spotted calf we both raised together had not escaped on her own; I opened the door for her to leave; that's why I hid myself when I found out that he found her at the bottom of a ravine. I had spent twenty-five years keeping it from him, and at that moment I remembered that and many, many other things that were burning me deep inside. Later came the Cristeros revolt, and I joined out of despair, without even knowing what we were fighting about. I found out that she was with the opposition and that she had become the big chief's lover. They began to light one cigarette after another, one bullet after another, without hitting the target. They considered me an idiot because I faced them unprotected. "Do you want to get killed?" I heard before they caught me. That's what I wanted, to end up in their hands, once and for all, to see if it's true that one can hear the crows caw; and I did it. I have only three hours left to fill with smoke or remorse.

"Give him some brandy so that he doesn't feel anything."

"All right, captain."

"I don't want him to suffer, those are the orders of Jacinta, *la Generala*."

22

Upon seeing Señora Rodríguez pregnant, Susanita cried out, "Mama, how was it possible?" Señora Rodríguez tried to explain how, as she knitted an adjustable maternity dress, and only managed to get entangled in the skein of yarn. With the hand that was free Señora Rodríguez tried to show Susanita that she was still young, drawing out of her purse the baby tooth that had fallen out the night she became pregnant. Señora Rodríguez felt doubly pregnant when Susanita explained to her: "What I mean is that it's not possible that you would be so foolish. You must know about contraceptives." Señora Rodríguez laughed through the teeth that she had left. She had gone through menopause five years before.

Fifteen months later, Baby Rodríguez was born, and from the time he emitted his first sound he proved to be a precocious child. Instead of crying he made fun of the doctor, the nurse, and his own mother. Moreover, he had all his teeth with the exception of the lower left canine, the same one that Señora Rodríguez had lost. At two months, Baby Rodríguez spoke his first word, which was not Mama, but Grandmother. Señora Rodríguez was in agreement and registered him as her grandson, son of an unknown mother. After putting the certificate away in her purse, next to those of Susanita and Carlitos, she commented to her husband, "It all turned out better than we had hoped for, right, darling?" and began to rub his head.

Heard in Passing

It would be great if life did not make us old, but all of a sudden the days appear completely wrinkled. The hours cram together and pass by all at once, two o'clock, three o'clock, four o'clock, and without one's realizing it, it's already dark; and one is stuck between a yellowish and used-up life, with a bunch of useless minutes where nothing happens because it has already happened. It's because sometimes we get a second-hand life that others have already lived. In my life someone has already beaten me to being a bullfighter, another married the wife that I wanted, another one became rich with my work, and there was even someone who died in my place. So I was left with nothing to do. And life is more and more dry and decayed. There are weeks that begin and do not end; Sundays repeat themselves endlessly because they lack the strength to become Mondays. And, if by chance they make it, they start at six in the afternoon, when the sun is already setting and women are covering up their birds, and the elderly remember their dead ones. Oh well, some of us have to live with a life that has been handled by others; I don't know how they manage to be the first ones and break it in. The only time that I saw dawn it was cloudy and the roosters didn't even sing, so I went back to sleep until my boss found out and fired me. I tried to explain it to her, and she acted as if she did not hear me. That's why I say that life resembles my boss, it passes in front of us without seeing us or hearing us, without stopping. And we see it leaving without living it. I've spent a lot of time watching it pass by, and each year I notice it's farther away, more filled with people who find no exit. And why not, if at this point, any end of a week, end of a month or year, joins up with the end of the century. Damned life, and then we don't want it to get old.

At the age of five Baby Rodríguez became independent. He ran away with his kindergarten teacher, a six-foot, twenty-year-old blond, whom he raped during recess after getting her drunk with a tequila-injected apple. Baby Rodríguez was accused of corrupting adults, an accusation from which he was freed on bail, paid by the blond, who couldn't live without him from that day on.

Together they set up a business selling objects made especially for precocious children. They sold fake birth certificates, fake mustaches, dentures for toothless children, platform tennis shoes, and all types of paraphernalia for making love before age ten. With the income they bought themselves a yacht and cruised around the world. "I wonder which side of the family he takes after?" Señora Rodríguez asked her husband, while taking an apple out of her purse and setting it on the table. Señor Rodríguez was reading the paper. The apple was red and shiny. Señor Rodríguez stopped reading the paper and crushed it. Señora Rodríguez blinked toward the apple. Señor Rodríguez felt that his underwear was too tight. The apple rolled to the floor. Señor Rodríguez grabbed it in a flash and devoured it with a single bite, spitting out the seed and taking off his pants. Señora Rodríguez was waiting for him under the table, laughing. That was the third apple Señor Rodríguez had eaten that day and there were still five left in her purse. "I don't know," answered Señor Rodríguez.

The Same Stock

To Carolina Aranda

They were two, man and woman, but two. And they looked with the look of the others, those who were not there. We knew that the man and the woman had stayed among us to listen to and to mock us and to take pleasure in watching us. I don't know how many we were, perhaps five, perhaps ten, however many we were, we were sitting in a circle with them in the middle, so we were not able to keep anything from them, nor speak without their hearing us.

The man and the woman talked only to each other, and it was as if everyone else, those who were not present, were there, just like before, with their lovely perfumed bodies. We seemed not to be there, also like before, while the others laughed and screamed and we remained silent. The man and the woman knew that as long as they were there, the others would also be there. That's why they remained in the same place, provoking the same distrust, the same uneasiness as always.

Every afternoon they arrived on time, and as they entered, it appeared as if they were coming from somewhere over there, and as they left, it appeared as if they were going toward somewhere over there. Perhaps someone was waiting for them and in this way, we all remained together, except they didn't let themselves be seen.

Then, one of us, the one we called "the deaf one," but really he was mute, fell in love with the woman. When he saw her he shrieked and masturbated in silence, despairing at being unable to speak. The old man, however, looked at the man and tears fell from his eyes, remembering who knows what. He cried without saying a word because no one paid attention to him, not even us, because he was old. Chachalaca was the only one who dared to go near them; she took a flower to the woman, who refused to take it from Chachalaca's deformed fingers, and we all went on hating each other. If they could have, they would have decapitated us, and if we had had the strength, we would have beaten them to take away their beauty. But we could do nothing but look at them from afar, and some of us couldn't even do that, for example, the blind man.

When the deaf one died, the woman started getting fat; after three months the woman's belly stuck out. The man, more than just her lover, behaved as if he were her bodyguard. She, on the other hand, was careful of her pregnancy as if she feared that someone, perhaps the others, would blame her if she didn't come full term.

The man and the woman continued attending our meetings and they forced us to be isolated. Although there were more of us, we remained at the edge of this transformation that was developing before our eyes and seized our attention. The body, bigger and bigger, gave the feeling that it was spying on us.

Today when we arrived they were already there, sitting in the same place; except that now, there were three of them.

24

Carlitos never met Baby Rodríguez: when the latter was born, the former had already left to see the world as a stowaway on a ship. Nevertheless, Carlitos and his brother were like two left socks. So much so that when they bumped into each other, one afternoon while walking on the sidewalk, they didn't realize that they were two, and they went off one behind the other, certain that they were one. From that day on, if Carlitos raised his left hand, Baby Rodríguez raised his right; if Baby Rodríguez closed his right eye, Carlitos imitated with his left and if one of them began to laugh, the other finished it. They looked at each other to comb their hair or brush their teeth and both went to sleep at the same time and dreamed the same thing. One time they almost discovered that they were two. It was when one of them woke up before the other, we don't know which one. What we do know is that the one who was awake thought he was still asleep, dreaming that he had awakened; while the one sleeping dreamed that he was dreaming he was awake; with which both were satisfied. They lived this way for a few months until one day, as they came to a corner, Carlitos turned to the right and Baby Rodríguez to the left, and they never saw each other again. Still, neither of them realized the disappearance of the other because they never knew about each other's existence. The only one who was upset about it was the blond teacher who did know which was which. Besides her, only Señora Rodríguez could tell them apart, by a birth mark that one of them has; but she jealously keeps this secret in her purse, along with the secret of the Virgin of Fátima, the map of the fountain of youth, and a picture of a young boy in love, which bears the following dedication: "To Señora Rodríguez from your fervent admirer: Dorian Gray."

At the Baptismal Font

That Sunday, when I arrived, I saw Relámpago still unsaddled. A lump came to my throat; by that time Don Antonio should have been on his way to Mezquital. I went around the back and entered through the back door; his voice stopped me halfway through the patio: "And you, where are you coming from?" That was all he said, and without waiting for a reply, he left, never to return. The loathing with which he looked at me was enough to make me break down. After a while I removed my shawl, and, controlling my shame, I continued cooking, straightening up the house, waiting for him.

I counted the days and nights. Yes, I missed his fast walk, his cigarette, his hat, his man's smell.

Don Antonio behaved as he should have with me, there was no reason for him to be any different. I was grateful to him for noticing me that afternoon at the fair. He, a full-grown man. I was sporting a new dress and shoes, and, why deny it, I flirted with him; I, too, was attracted. I agreed to dance with him even if it angered Ramón, the brother of my friend Lupe, who was just a kid. What happened was that Don Antonio took me into his home. There, I turned fifteen. He told me that his first wife had died of a miscarriage, it was the only thing I found out about her.

At first I felt happy to be his wife, then two years had passed, and we still had no children. I began to fear that he would leave me because I didn't give him a child, but how could I, if whenever it was time he wouldn't come near me. I thought that he didn't want me to die like his first wife; although I also imagined that he already had another woman and he put up with me out of pity. But as soon as we were together I forgot about everything, since he did it with such eagerness that he ended up convincing me. I would say each time: "Now it will happen," but nothing did. And I kept on taking remedies and asking the Virgin to send us at least one child. The townspeople now were looking at me out of the corner of their eye and gossiping about me, saying I wasn't a woman, that I was useless, and they would stare at my stomach. At my age I should have been a mother already, just like all the others. The last straw was that Lupe, my best friend, said that Don Antonio didn't love me. I ran to church to pray that my husband would give me a child so that I could silence everyone, one by one.

That morning, while going to seven o'clock mass, Ramón caught up with me.

"Edelmira," he stopped me, "Don't you remember your old friends any more?"

I remembered. His voice hadn't changed, on the contrary, he . . .

"Yes Ramón," I answered. "I heard that you were up north."

"Well, I'm back."

I swear to you, Father, that that was the only time. At that moment, if it hadn't been Sunday, Don Antonio should have been on his way to Mezquital. It was an opportunity to prove myself. "If I get pregnant, I can make him believe that it's his and he'll be happy," I thought, not remembering what day it was.

Yesterday they brought me his body slung across Relámpago. They say that they saw him roaming around Ramón's ranch many times until a shootout occurred between them. They said that it was because of some problem about land; and the two of them shot each other. No one knows the truth. I didn't know either that Don Antonio wasn't capable, nor that he killed his first wife for being unfaithful. But you did know it, Father, and you kept it from me when I asked you to bless me so that I could have children. You also deceived me, as I did him, so baptize him now for me and name him Antonio. Only you and I will know that he is Ramón's son.

25

Fifteen years ago, at the same moment that Carlitos was peeing on the new sofa and Susanita was screaming because she had gotten her finger stuck in the door, Señora Rodríguez received a posthumous letter from her Aunt Clotilde. After putting the letter away in her purse for "later," she pinched Susanita and made Carlitos's finger better. Today she came across that letter under her mother-in-law's dentures, between Lady Windermere's fan and the Amozocian rosary. "How I like to receive news," said Señora Rodríguez while opening the envelope:

"Dearest niece:

I hope that this letter finds you well. At eighty years I couldn't be better, you'll see why.

Remember that little mole I had on my left arm? Well, it turned into a little pimple. A fact which would've been of no importance had it stayed that way, but no, the pimple kept growing, minute by minute, and in a short time it had become a monumental zit. One early morning I awoke to find it staring at me: In the middle of the zit two diminutive eyes, just like mine, were watching me. I opened my eyelids wider, wishing to see them better and the little eyes also widened without interrupting their gaze. With difficulty I got into a long-sleeved dress, being careful so that I didn't hurt the eyes. I decided to wait. The next morning, below the eyes I recognized a nose identical to mine, which I had to blow with one of my hankies from Brussels. It seemed to have a cold and I wasn't about to let it stain the silk blouse that Porfirio gave me. Another day passed and a mouth appeared, with a tiny, light mustache, right above the upper lip, exactly like mine. It's more than enough to say that during these months I've been thinking a lot about Porfirio, he would've been so happy. The only problem was to hide what was happening to me. The sleeve got tighter and tighter and the tickles which the little tongue gave me made me laugh in the least appropriate places. Nevertheless, I was content. The mouth now would smile at me and soon it would utter its first word. I anxiously hoped that an arm would sprout forth, then another, then the body, the legs. What would it be, a boy or a girl?

I've spent the last weeks indoors harboring my secret. There's little time left now. 'Perhaps tomorrow,' I think, looking at the photograph that Porfirio gave me sixty years ago. If he only knew that it has a wart on its inner thigh exactly like him. . . ."

A Time of Mourning

To Don Joaquín Díez-Canedo Mortiz

Now I know that Joaquín was twenty years older than Sofía, an inequality that she softened under the downy lip of a small-town woman, with tortoiseshell combs on each side of her head and a generously sized apron. But back then it was difficult for me to guess how old Sofía was, always behind the iron entry gate, receiving bread in the morning, or watering the garden in the afternoon. Her husband, on the other hand, came and went in his car, which was driven by a chauffeur who called him "Don Joaquín" as he opened the door with a bend of the waist, which made his employer appear to be much taller than he really was. The car bore Joaquín away, leaving the carport open, an opportunity that his wife took advantage of to peek secretively out into the street before closing it.

Sofía spoke only with children. Amongst ourselves we remarked that she spoke by singing and that she ended her words with either "u" or "i," from which the adults determined the couple's place of origin: "So far as I'm concerned they come from Michoacán," my mother said. "No, it's in Tepa where they speak like that," contradicted my father. "Except they look like the people in Uruapan and if they make guava jelly, surely that's where they're from." I never learned how to differentiate between one place and another, just as I didn't know how to differentiate between a woman who was pregnant and one who wasn't. So I spent many years waiting for Sofía to have a child, and she never had one.

When they arrived, there were many of us children on the block. We all used to pass by the house on the corner to go to the store, but none of us got to know the new neighbors the way I did. First I became friends with the cat, which I picked up one day when he was lost. I asked at various homes if it was theirs, until the only house left was the one on the corner. I knocked with my nine years palpitating inside of me; Sofía opened the door. It was the first time she ever offered me cookies and tea. It was her cat, it couldn't have been anyone else's: black, completely black.

The mysteries about the couple began to disturb me when I found out that Joaquín had died. The wake was held with so much discretion that no one noticed Sofía's sadness, dressed as she always was. Nevertheless, behind her thick and long eyelashes hid a reserved cunning, the kind we had on Good Friday, when we went to church only for the meatless pastries. Joaquín died precisely on Holy Thursday without affecting that week of mourning. When Easter arrived no one remembered him anymore: Sofía, like a reminiscence of herself, continued watering the garden, making guava jelly, and looking down the street from afar, under her thick eyebrows, which accentuated her widowhood.

Sofía's house faced onto two streets and, from both, one could see her sitting behind a window, embroidering, knitting, attending to her memories, wrapped in a black robe.

The second time I entered her house, making my way through the flower pots filled with ferns and multicolored cages, I found her talking to the canaries. Her hands, extremely white, trembled under the yellowish wings of two chicks whose mother had died. She looked at me without releasing the birds and said: "Joaquín promised me that you would come sooner or later. Come in." Then she led me to the living room and served a boiling cup of tea which I drank in sips. Sitting in front of me, she observed me, lightly touching my skin with her look.

I went back the next morning, the next and the next, trapped by Sofía's long eyelashes or by the clamor of her hands, or by her way of saying things as if she were singing. Without protesting I helped her knit baby clothes, embroider and prepare a basket for a baby. She, meanwhile, talked about her life with Joaquín, placing his picture below the erratic light given off by a candle which sparked reflections in Sofía's hair.

At first my house was three houses away from hers, then two, then one, and finally I found myself looking through her gate. I didn't realize at what point I learned to differentiate between the herbs of fecundation and those of rejuvenation, but one evening I caught myself invoking the spirit of love and drinking out of Sofía's cup. I never thought she could go beyond making tea, lighting candles, and mixing herbs, but in time, I realized that an unknown Sofía took hold of her and me in the waning hours of daylight. "Joaquín assured me that I would never be alone again," she exclaimed, with conviction, and I repeated her words without remembering who had said them first, she or I.

One early morning I woke up thinking of Joaquín, as I might have known him long ago, before I was born: and it's because the night before I had dreamed about him, he was calling me Joaquín. I explained to him that I wasn't him, he was mistaken. Without recognizing me, he kept calling me Joaquín. When I told Sofía about it, she wasn't surprised: I had an identical dream, she said, and then we both started humming the same song with no forethought. From that day on, if she gets hurt I feel it; if I'm hungry, Sofía eats and I feel satisfied. Nor can we keep anything from each other; I know that Sofía awaits the new moon, which is the day I'll turn fifteen, to carry out her plan: each nightfall she practices her nuptials all alone, laying naked her widowhood little by little; then her flesh is filled with diminutive tongues that cover her from head to toe.

Today we woke up singing, certain that Sofía will not menstruate for nine months, at which time, with her own hand, she will cut our baby's umbilical cord. At twilight, as I straightened out the bird's cage where the female laid her eggs, I began to desire her. We went to the bedroom, closed the windows, and turned off the lights. The edges of the night clung to her mouth, darkening it. Nocturnal words, kept silent by day, awoke the silence, filling it with suggestions, with demands, with anxiousness. Sofía opened her body to desire, stripping off her clothes and covering herself with dreams and making the new moon grow in me, until our hands and legs were united in one single longing: Sofía's, who feverishly pronounced Joaquín's name with more and more vehemence. Just like in the dream, I screamed to her that I wasn't him, that she was mistaken. Sofía seemed not to hear me; at last, she proclaimed: "It has to be this way."

In front of Joaquín's picture we loved and hated each other at the same time, and all my repressed passions exploded with fury in her womb.

Now I know that Sofía is twenty years older than I; that under her apron, her skin is infinite, and from now on we will always share the same sorrow: Sofía thinks of Joaquín: I, of her.

26

Señora Rodríguez built herself a two-by-two world where there was only enough room for her. The world was round and shielded, transparent and aseptic. Everyone could see Señora Rodríguez sitting in a papal chair, which one day was placed on Europe, the next day on America, the following day on Africa, and so on. Señora Rodríguez, purse on shoulder, greeted those who were outside by wrinkling her nose. The world of Señora Rodríguez tirelessly revolved on its own axis until a small child peered between Oceania and the Falkland Islands and asked, "Excuse me, are you Señora Padilla?" Señora Rodríguez tried to change course, but the steering did not obey. Drawn to its own likeness, the world went spinning toward an enormous mirrored wall that reflected it, and it smashed against itself. Both collapsed in a clatter of broken eggshells.

In the middle of the debris Señora Rodríguez found her best friend, dead; her favorite professor, the one who had betrayed her; her first high-heeled shoes; her forgotten Aunt Clotilde. . . . Señora Rodríguez gathered all the fragments and placed them in her purse inside a match box. When Señor Rodríguez took it out to light a cigarette, all the little pieces of the world had gone bad. "This woman and her mania for collecting junk," growled Señor Rodríguez, hurling the match box into the garbage.

Last Night, Mariana

To Marisa Díez-Canedo

When I first met Mariana she did nothing but cry, eat, and sleep. She had blond hair and blue eyes, just like mine, and we were the same size, except she wore diapers and I wore lace underwear with pink bows. I also wore patent leather shoes and hers were knitted. She was so helpless that I fell in love with her and didn't realize that she had begun to grow. Nevertheless, she had not yet learned to talk. I, on the other hand, said ma-ma when I was tipped forward. That's how Mariana learned. Then she said papa, tita, bow-wow, and baby. Ever since then that's what she called me. Mariana was soft and warm and had downy fuzz on her face.

Mariana had a little brother; his name is Toño and he looks like her, although Mariana says that he is very ugly and wants him to be sent back. Her parents gave her a puppy so that she would forget about him, but she didn't. Every time that her mother nurses Toño, Mariana cuddles with me and whispers in my ear: "Don't worry, I will never give you a little brother."

The day before yesterday I didn't see Mariana for quite a while. Very early in the morning they brushed her hair into a ponytail, put an apron on her, and gave her a kiss. When she returned she had colored pencils and a coloring book. "Look," she showed me, "I know how to make an A." Yesterday she returned crying, with her knees scraped. "Kids are very mean," she told me. In the afternoons we play house or school. She's always the teacher.

Mariana has fat fingers that are somewhat clumsy, she has trouble buttoning up my dress, after twisting my arms trying to put it on. Now we only play on Mondays, the other days she has ballet classes, piano classes, swimming or English classes. Sometimes she gives me a bath on Saturdays, if she doesn't have to go to her grandma's house. From the shelf where I spend the week, I see her come home daily. She leaves me sitting but I lean sideways little by little, until I end up crooked, fallen over to one side, waiting for Mariana to come and straighten me up or to open my eye, which shuts every time she runs out and slams the door. Here I can feel the walls resound as buses pass by, and I know if somebody is coming by the bark Blackie makes. I also know if Mariana is happy with herself: she looks at herself in the mirror and smiles, in spite of her lack of teeth. She does this when she wears new shoes, a new dress, or when she blows bubbles with her gum. If she's angry she looks at herself out of the corner of her eye and lowers her head, then she hides her feet under the blankets and begins to cover herself completely, slowly, as if she were looking for herself.

Last night Mariana fell asleep with great sighs and sucking her thumb. At midnight she woke up and took me in with her. She was sad because she was left alone with her grandma; her parents had gone on a trip. We lay down on their bed for a while. Mariana says that their pillows smell good, but they had changed the sheets and the pillow cases smelled like detergent. Mariana cried and said, "I think God is imprisoned because He doesn't pay any attention to me." Her grandma asked her, "Who are you talking to, Mariana?"

Mariana hasn't cried again; every day she talks more on the telephone and less with me. When she goes to bed she no longer prays like she used to. She falls asleep listening to music. She has also changed from patent leather shoes to tennis shoes, and when she laughs, she shows her braces. She looks so pretty with jeans and her wild hair that she wants to become an actress. "Comb your hair," orders her mother, who knows nothing about fashions. "Comb your own hair," Mariana answers, locking herself up in the bathroom and applying more hair spray. "Mothers are very mean," Mariana writes on the fogged-up mirror when she showers.

Mariana hit me. They had punished her for getting bad grades by not letting her watch TV. She looked at me, called me stupid and threw me to the floor. It was the last time I said ma-ma. Then, Mariana took out a picture of a boy and cut it up with some scissors into many pieces. First she cut off his hands, next his legs, then his head and finally she poked a hole in his heart. "Men are very mean," she cried, picking up all the pieces and putting them back together as if it were a puzzle, and added: "He'll see when they take these damn things off my teeth."

Mariana did not go to school because she had an exam. She pretended she had a stomachache and stayed in bed. At noon she woke up yelling, "They're going to flunk me," and, since she had nothing to do, she started to clean the closet. I was happy waiting for my turn to be dusted. "Here I am," I thought from the corner where Mariana had put me the last time she was punished. Mariana took out her skateboard, her old book bags, her clips of movie stars, her First Communion dress, and her tennis rackets. "Pretty soon now," I gave myself hope watching the sliver of light where all the things were going out. All of a sudden I felt a pull and, along with some worn-out shoes and a deflated ball, I landed on the bottom of the trash can. "To the trash," exclaimed Mariana. Do you suppose it's because I no longer say ma-ma?

Señora Rodríguez left her house. When she passed by the house right next door, she didn't recognize it. "They must have had it remodeled last night," she assumed, continuing on her way. She thought the same thing about the dog across the street, and she went on thinking it about all the neighbors on her block. At the corner she saw that the street name had changed: "Champs Elysées," it sounds familiar, she thought, and crossed over to the other sidewalk. Further ahead, Señora Rodríguez realized she was in a different city from her own when she heard herself being greeted in French. "Bonjour," she responded, happy to have studied French in twenty lessons. "One never knows," she had said. Señora Rodríguez started to suspect that something was not right when she noticed that the people were dressed according to the fashion of the beginning of the century. Señora Rodríguez took out a calendar from her purse, just in case, and was surprised to see that it was a French calendar from 1912. "I grabbed the wrong purse again," she exclaimed, returning home. But she did not find it. It was her Aunt Clotilde's purse, and in 1912 Señora Rodríguez still hadn't been born.

Without existing, Señora Rodríguez traveled all over the world, was a witness to history, and taking advantage of not being seen, modified the facts as she pleased, after donating her aunt's purse to a museum so that in the future something like that wouldn't happen to her again. But above all, she tracked down the herd from which the cow had come, whose skin her purse would be manufactured from. She discovered the quality and durability of the hide and calculated its duration before her mother-in-law dreamed of giving the purse to her. The purse was already very shabby at the time Señora Rodríguez switched it with Aunt Clotilde's and realized that she wouldn't be able to keep it for very long. Fortunately, since the date of her birth was approaching, Señora Rodríguez was gradually forgetting everything, until it was all completely erased when she let out her first cry. In a similar way, upon approaching chapter 28, Señora Rodríguez felt insecure, without knowing why.

It's Their Fault

To Ernesto Flores

Did you hear the snap of your vertebrae? Did you hear it? It was right after the scream, or at the same time. You should know better; although perhaps not, because at that moment you became deaf. The scream and the crack exploded while your legs dangled near the weeds. You felt the pressure of the rope on your neck and the blood pumping into your sex, while your legs dangled. You let your fingers relax their grip and urinated, while your legs dangled. You realized that you would not be able to scream again, while your legs dangled, while your legs dangled.

While your legs dangled, you daydreamed about Esther, that she put figs in your mouth. Sweet figs that blended with her lips, with her tongue, with your name pronounced in intervals; saturating your senses with her skin, with her breath, with her aroma, in exchange for your doing what she asked of you; and you, letting yourself be convinced by her persuasive hands, which came and went up the ladder of pleasure. The last doubt disappeared when she told you that, furthermore, she would pay you to do it. With that money you would buy perfumes and fabrics to anoint her, wrap and unwrap her each night. . . .

While your legs dangled you recalled, you did not recall, you recalled a kiss, that other kiss with which you were going to pay for hers. Thirty dinars of sweet figs just for pointing out the Messiah, anyone would have done it if Esther had asked.

He did not resist and was easily captured. You ran to give Esther the news. You were thinking of her, of what she would tell you with her mouth, with her eyes, with her hands. . . . You had managed to forget about yourself, your childhood, your mother who believed you were perfect and wished you were rich and famous. Nor did you remember that you had grown up among yes's and no's: "Yes, I can, no, I shouldn't, is it okay?" Upon your mother's death you swore that you would become someone. She expected so much of you that you couldn't disappoint her, she was the only woman worthy of your affection, before you met Esther. Until then you didn't believe yourself capable of loving anything but power and money. To obtain both you joined up with the king of the Jews. Immediately you realized that he didn't have anything you didn't have. Except the disciples did not follow you; on the contrary, they looked at you with distrust; and all for what, if it so happens that his kingdom is not of this world, and you believing that you were the governor of some province, after freeing your village from the Romans. Yes, you were ambitious. How else can one escape mediocrity? Esther was right, you're the only intelligent one among your peers, you and she, so she wasn't going to wait around for you to decide whether to stay with her or with the Master. Esther always knew what she wanted. Oh, what envy to know what one wants, because the Master, the Master loved you, and you did not want to bring him any harm, even though Esther convinced you to do the opposite. If only he had not been so . . . so different from you. Where did he get those ideas? And then he also knew how to attract the crowds and even heal them. Or were they tricks? Perhaps he was in league with the sick people, yes, that must have been it. While your legs dangle you relive the time you tried to heal some blind man and weren't able, and out of rage you felt like killing the Master. More than one had probably felt the same way, that's why they followed him, it wasn't just because he went around proclaiming he was the son of God. No one even believed him. Well, those who didn't know him, but surely, the son of God? No, you imagined God differently. After all, if he weren't who he claimed to be, let them punish him for being a fake, and if he were, we would find out. Esther said it well: "Yes, it's true, he will not allow anything to happen to himself, don't worry." Esther, what would she have done if you had been the Messiah? And you, what would you have done yourself? Don't think about it anymore, it was necessary to eliminate him, it was the only way you could get ahead, and she would be proud of you. If you hadn't accepted the deal you would have lost her, you would have lost her and you would have gone mad. If you were capable of hanging yourself from a tree, you would be capable of that. Esther, so much like your mother . . .

When you arrived with the news, you heard them, their outbursts of laughter could be heard outside. Then you heard the man's voice as he was leaving: "We no longer need him. Esther, get rid of him; from now on he'll just be in the way. And take the money from him, thirty dinars isn't a lot, but we could use them." Your hands trembled as you opened the door: The whiteness of her naked body blinded you. You didn't look when you strangled her, nor when you fell to your knees before her to spit at her and kiss her and forgive her and despise her and kiss her again and ask her forgiveness. She did not answer.

At nightfall you started on your way to the field. You chose a branch. The fact that Esther had deceived you, you alone, you couldn't stand. It was her fault; and the disciples for being distrustful; and the Master for not understanding you; and your mother for bringing you into the world; and the one who bribed you, all, all are GUILTY . . . screamed your scream while your legs dangled.

Afterward you left your mouth wide open for a few minutes, as if waiting for the scream to finish coming out; but the scream was already on its way, filled with you. The audacity with which you hurled it joined it and ended up caught in the tree or on the shore of the night. And you were biting your tongue until it was bitten through. And a scream is not just a scream. Years of repression have accumulated in your throat and are expelled by your entire body, with all the frustration of not being the son of God, with all the humiliation of the "farewells" that turned you into a "cuckold" to those who watched you smile when you said farewell to her, instead of screaming like you did today. It's better to scream on time, before someone beats us to it; even though it is not easy. The scream is carried inside because it only serves, at the most, for some idiot to scoff at when he sees us with our eyes bulging from the effort and our veins swollen from the excitement. That is to say, the scream exhausts itself for lack of breath and rage to hurl another.

The long chain of why's that was suffocating you, when you arrived at "why was I born," broke and liberated your consciousness. Your legs have stopped in the middle of the silence. Now you have an empty mind, that is all.

28

Señora Rodríguez was feeling confused. She would open her purse and would invariably find Carlitos's pacifier, Susanita's gum, the recipe for bread pudding, the sandalwood rosary, the hanky from Brussels, the balloons, the party favors, or the contraceptives; but she could never find herself. "This is a fraud, I'll put an end to this farce"; and with her mind made up to end it all, Señora Rodríguez started looking in her purse, where she only found dots and dashes, new paragraphs, a colon, a semicolon, and ellipsis, and no final period. "I must take further measures," Señora Rodríguez decided as she put her foot in her purse. That way, when she opened it, the first thing she'd see would be her face. . . . And who would open it, if she was inside? she reflected when she was inside up to her chin. With difficulty, she emerged, dragging with her Carlota Pérez's crinolines. Señora Rodríguez put them away and continued meditating: "I've got it!" she said excitedly to herself, "from now on I'll be Mrs. Smith."

Mrs. Smith delightedly opened her purse and found Charlie's pacifier, Susy's gum, the recipe for apple pie, the . . .

Right Place, Wrong Time

Lucky number, eight; favorite color, green; birthstone, ruby. Tomorrow you will receive a surprise."

Tomorrow, forced to wait until tomorrow once more. Why do things always happen the day after? Tomorrow I will not be me because I will be one day older, a day less young; I will have seen what I have not seen today and heard what I have not heard before; what other surprise can there be? Although . . . perhaps tomorrow I will be able to meet someone who is now in Rome or Berlin and doesn't know that I am here, hoping that he buys a plane ticket to Mexico, gets on board twenty minutes before twelve, fastens his seat belt, reads the "No Smoking" sign every time it lights up during the flight, until finally he descends and lands among one hundred other passengers, takes a taxi that brings him to me, and asks me how to find a certain street, unaware that, since prehistoric times, in Rome or in Berlin, all the factors were coinciding so that one day, tomorrow, a blond man with gray eyes, almost six feet tall and with one foot shorter than the other and a scar on his stomach, would meet me at one of the four corners of the globe and would ask me if he should turn right or left. In the meantime, I had to be born in this place exactly thirty years, two months, five days, fifteen minutes, and ten seconds ago, so that at this moment I answer him: left. He, in fact, turns to the left following my instructions, after saying thank you, I have an important meeting and I must be punctual. And I don't know whether to stop him and explain to him that one of us is wrong; that his today is my tomorrow, that I can still leave so that I won't be here when he arrives, that he should not decide for me the date I will find him; that he went ahead or that I lived anticipating what I was planning for later, with him, and this means that I didn't live one day, but which one? . . . I would need to be reborn, to newly review each moment that draws me to this one and see where I failed; because otherwise, the blond man with gray eyes, almost six feet tall and with the scar on his stomach and one foot shorter than the other, will go to a meeting he can never make.

Looking in her purse for the bread pudding recipe, Señora Rodríguez discovered the manuscript of the book, *Señora Rodríguez.* Then it is true that I do not exist, she moaned. But she immediately rectified her statement: Then it is true that I do exist. Señora Rodríguez wanted to know what she was like (and so did I); unfortunately in the text she did not find precise data. The way I see it, she deduced, I have to paint myself on my own. And she began to put on a straight nose, a thick mouth, and ample hips, below a robust waist. She colored her hair brown and curly and the eyebrows arched, and lastly, she put a mole near her lower lip, on the left side. Señora Rodríguez continued looking through the manuscript and lost her color when she realized that she had become pregnant at fifty-five. She lost her smell when she saw that the baby had run away with his kindergarten teacher, and lost her taste when she found out that she was going to die on page 134. Señora Rodríguez began to cry. The first thing that faded away were her eyes, then her nose and mouth. Seeing that the ink stain continued to run, Señora Rodríguez folded the paper, put it in her purse, and just in case, hid a pen between her breasts. Next time, she sighed, I'll make myself blond.

Blame It on Hormones

To Agustín Monsreal

She had always been lucky; this explains why, in forty years, she got the measles in her thirties and apart from that had never been ill, had surgery, or even had a late period. Nor could she complain of greater misfortunes except for the death, due to old age, of her paternal grandmother and the stubbornness of her husband, of which, knowing how to handle it, she could make the most. In summary, this was her life when she first became aware of the discomfort.

She had spent her end-of-the-year vacation on the beach and the circumstances appeared to indicate that the new year would be as satisfactory as the previous year and the year previous to that, and all the previous ones since 1960 until today. Except for the small irritation on her nose, she felt vigorous and had an enormous desire to mark 1990 with a party. The crisis could wait until she got old, and that was far from happening. She confirmed this by putting on some sweatpants and going out to run. Once or twice she scratched her nose unconsciously, the third time she looked at her hand so closely that she thought, "I should paint my nails," before scratching; and then dropped the subject.

Her tan generally lasted without fading up to a week after she returned, so she planned the party for the following Saturday. It would take her three days to call her friends, fix the house, and prepare the dinner. Perhaps she would get a new carpet, "New year, new life," was her slogan, although in reality her existence had not varied much in those years. On some occasions she thought that no matter how fortunate she was, she would always have a problem, but right away she forgot about it and continued to enjoy life without any remorse about her situation: good service, an excellent husband — she scratched her nose — and adorable children, she acknowledged, when she finished scratching.

On Saturday night she picked a dress that contrasted with the tone of her skin, touched up her makeup and went down to welcome her guests. She liked to have a special comment for each guest: Marcela's suit fits her very well; Nora's earrings are marvelous, surely they were a Christmas present. Silvia had lost weight, and . . . again the itching of her nose, which distracted her from admiring Ivette's new necklace.

The reunion progressed happily, while her nose gained importance. She could no longer avoid feeling it, in spite of Ricardo's dirty jokes. Perhaps the cigarette smoke was irritating her; she went as far as asking Nora if the tip of her nose was getting red. Nora didn't see anything, maybe she had been in the sun too long, and soon the irritation would disappear.

The next day, however, the irritation continued, even though it wasn't visible. "That's enough," she told herself, and decided to put some ointment on it. When she showed up with the white ointment everyone stared: Mom using medicine? Leave that to Dad who had already had hepatitis and typhoid fever, or to Uncle Quico who was always breaking his bones; she didn't have the right to disappoint her children who had never heard her complain from even a toothache. She ran to wipe it off and did not mention the itch again. To disguise the itching she began to blow her nose repeatedly: "Mom, do you have a cold?" her children cried, as if she had acquired leprosy.

Until now she had been very proud of her straight nose, which began to look sort of round due to the little blackhead. Yes, it was a blackhead, probably a pimple. And at her age. The thought of being ridiculed went through her mind without settling, it was nothing to worry about, yet, although it was getting on her nerves.

She spent the rest of the afternoon looking for a solution: first she'd have to extract the pus from the pimple without bruising it. She needed to steam the affected spot to open the pores so that the contents would run out. She boiled water and poured it in a bowl and placed her towel-covered head over the steam. She did everything herself to make sure every step was correct. Once the necessary steps were done she took two handkerchiefs and extracted the blackhead. "I've had enough, no more zits," she thought while she squeezed her nose with her fingernails. It had been too easy, the pus came out clean, followed by a drop of blood. She focused on the point through a magnifying mirror which allowed her to see it perfectly clear . . . another one! This time on the forehead. The thought that an acne invasion would affect her face set in her mind. It began with that horrible blackhead on her nose, and now her forehead. Who could say she wasn't going to end up disfigured? She couldn't spend her entire life waiting for each zit to mature in order to extract it. Then she thought of all the thousands of liters of water she'd have to boil to steam her face, the amount of tissue she'd use, and her swollen face the day the pimples came out from each pore of her skin. The tragedy took on a life of its own. It became the subject of conversation and even an excuse for her to come near her husband that night and, after telling him she couldn't sleep, she dared take the initiative. Yes, it's true that that nightmare never left her mind. She felt capable of confronting the consequences of this act. Nevertheless, as she touched the softness of his mouth, she remembered the eruption, the one that would surely end up separating them. How could he feel attracted to her? She decided to take drastic measures: she would go to a dermatologist and demand that he cure her as soon as possible. Of course this involved costs, loss of time, discomfort, but anything was better than being rejected. She knew that the dermatologist would examine her and ask indiscreet questions: Was she satisfied with her sex life? How often did she defecate? How old was she and did she have a normal menstruation? only to end up telling her that he'd try to help her without guaranteeing anything. She would come out of the office with scheduled hours to take medicine and instructions on how to wash her face, whether to eat or not eat, to return in fifteen days, and, at the end of that time period, she would not only be the same, but her nerves would be shot. If the treatment did not work, which was more than likely, another diagnosis would be necessary. Perhaps it was not just a simple case of acne. She had heard of certain types of cancer that began with the same symptoms. Better yet, the best thing would be to go directly to a pathologist.

A week had gone by since the appearance of that gruesome spot, and each day she was worse. She no longer dared to be seen in public without a good dose of make-up and an even better answer to those insistent questions. She couldn't stand Nora's stare, which was somewhere between sympathy and mockery. Nor impertinent Ivette with her brand-new plastic surgery. Would plastic surgery help her? First the tissue of cancer needed to be discarded. Yes, that's what it was without a doubt, and they would try to keep it from her the same way they did to poor Aunt Idalia. "How much time do I have to live? Aunt Idalia died believing she had tonsillitis, how naive. They won't fool me. No wonder they treat me with such pity, I must disgust them. And what if there were some remedy? Science is very advanced. No it's useless, I won't allow them to experiment on me as if I were a rabbit. Poor Aunt Idalia. Now I understand her. I won't let the same thing happen to me, I'll leave everything so my husband won't be able to marry someone else. Silvia, that slut, is always staring at him, and he's not one to let himself be courted. I'll fix that. It's an advantage knowing that one is going to die, that the funeral can be planned. They'll see what it's like to be left without a mother. I can imagine how my friends will react. Ivette will say: 'It was about time.' Silvia will be desperately awaiting my burial. Nora will probably remember me for a week. And to think that when we got married, he was the one who had the pimples. . . ."

"Darling?"

"Yes."

"I need to speak with you, it's useless for you to fake it, I know everything, and before I die you're going to listen to me."

"Is it your premenstrual pimple again?"

"How do you know?"

"Where?"

"On my forehead."

"I mean where would you like it, right here?"

30

Señora Rodríguez, in the grip of an existential crisis since discovering the manuscript of *Señora Rodríguez* in her purse, began to ask herself: "Who am I? Where did I come from? Where am I going?" and arrived at the following conclusion: The author put the manuscript in my purse because the author and I are the same person. Therefore I am the author of the author; without me she would not exist. And, doing it as she spoke, she took the manuscript from her purse and burned it. Señora Rodríguez was consumed in a second, fortunately she managed to let go of her purse on time. When Señor Rodríguez opened it, he took out a xerox copy of *Señora Rodríguez* which she had saved "just in case," and began to read it. Upon arriving at the twelfth line of page 125, Señor Rodríguez took the xerox copy of *Señora Rodríguez* from the purse and began to read it. Upon arriving at the twelfth line of page 125, Señor Rodríguez took the xerox copy of *Señora Rodríguez* from the purse and began to read it. Upon arriving at the twelfth line of page 125, Señor Rodríguez took the xerox copy of *Señora Rodríguez* from the purse and began to read it, upon arriving at the twelfth line of page 125 Señor Rodríguez took the xerox copy of *Señora Rodríguez* from the purse and began to read it, upon arriving at the twelfth line of page 125, Señor Rodríguez took the xerox copy of *Señora Rodríguez* from the purse and began to read it, upon arriving at the twelfth line of page 125, Señor Rodríguez took the xerox copy of *Señora Rodríguez* from the purse and began to read it, upon arriving at the twelfth line of page . . . 125.

Amanda's Motives

Today I turn fifty-three, said Raúl, caressing the recently purchased book. The cover was blue, and on the back cover Amanda smiled as she did from the other end of the table. Raúl returned the smile with a wink.

Amanda set a place for Irma and Laura who were just arriving.

"Luis is the only one missing," Raúl pointed out without anyone asking. Amanda did not answer. Luis would arrive. . . . Amanda kept looking at herself on the book cover. She had gone to a professional photographer; it was her first book, and she wanted to appear younger. The camera's lens filter made it possible.

"You look very good," Raúl had told her an hour earlier, "I like low-cut dresses."

She looked attractive and she knew it, and now Raúl, fifty-three years old, made her feel better.

"Do you know what we're celebrating?" Amanda asked, raising her glass.

"The publication of your book," everyone answered.

"No, Raúl's birthday."

Luis sat on the only empty seat which was next to Raúl. When Amanda saw them, Raúl was raising his glass.

"Well, yes, today is my birthday, how do I look? A few months ago they thought I had cancer; it was horrible, fortunately they were wrong."

"Then, what are you worrying about, it's a good thing you're still coming and going. What about your book?" asked Luis sipping his beer and patting Raúl's shoulder.

Raúl was speechless for a moment, then finally he spoke: "I hope next year, I'm sure."

Amanda, from the other end, kept an eye on the blue book which gradually began to blend in with the dishes and the tablecloth.

The newspaper articles rated Amanda's book between good and excellent. The cover was featured a few times in the papers until it began to blend in with the other books, just like it did on the table. In response Amanda brought out some colorful posters, enlarged, and placed them on the walls of her house.

"Who encouraged you to publish?" she was asked in an interview. Amanda recalled her first poems, her courtships: Alfonso, José, Luis. . . . Her marriages: Luis, Alfonso, José. That's what had encouraged her, life, in which she was the unopened letter. She had to bet on Amanda against all odds and against everyone. Literature became her husband and her lover. In it she invested her dreams, her experiences as a woman. Only now she found herself empty. A book is a high-risk birth, and Alfonso, Luis and José appeared in it; pages 36, 50, and 82, in that order.

Raúl arrived with some papers under his arm. They were a few poems written twenty years ago that had won a prize in a contest and had been published in a yellowish magazine that included Raúl's picture, before Raúl.

"How are you?"

"Fine, Amanda, thank you," Raúl said, showing her the papers. "I'd like you to give me the address and phone number of the publisher where you published; I'm going to finish my book. I'm writing again."

"Of course, Raúl, call me later."

Raúl left with the papers under his arm.

Page 36

He never did it; he would have made an attempt, but he was faint-hearted. I don't know why I loved him and lived so many years in his shadow, resigning myself to tasteless dedications, in the prime of my virginity. Alfonso, if indecision had a name, it would be "Alfonso." . . .

"Amanda, it's Raúl. Hey, give me the publisher's address, see I've already finished the book. It was very difficult. Remember my poems, the ones I won a prize for? Yes, the ones that were published in that magazine. Do you really like them? What did you say? Oh, yeah, I'll hurry, thanks for everything. Hey, if something comes up don't forget to invite me."

Page 50

Then I met Luis. He wasn't what I thought he would be, but he entertained me. I liked feeling protected by him. I began to write, motivated by Alfonso, by his suggestions, for him and because of him. Luis did not know it.

The blue cover was fading along with Amanda. The euphoria of the first days was growing bleak, and the book was no longer a goal. Once again everyday things appeared in her life, except now they were seen through a microscope. She'd have to find herself again in the anonymous and rivalrous multitude. Was it possible to stop being a writer from one day to the next? She saw Irma, Laura, and all those who still struggled to publish. A compulsion distinguished them from others, just like Raúl with his poems under his arm, showing them to the first person he could and at the age of fifty-three. His wife threatened to leave him, his health was weakening, but he had a reason to live. She, on the other hand, if her book wasn't successful, would have the beginning and the end of her career. How many had believed in her? How many had followed her example? How many had fallen into the trap?

Amanda opened the book to

> *Page 82*
>
> José's hand clung to my hand. Luis was next to me, he did not notice it. José, fifteen years older than me, was the third corner along with Alfonso and Luis. After so many years he seemed so interested, much more than before. What did he see in me, the forbidden woman, the young girl of the past? The truth is his wooing pleased me, I know he would have liked to have had an affair with me. He, such a gentleman, so decent, so cynical, holding me tight in front of my husband. . . .

"Mom, Bibiana is fighting with me, she wants to be the only one who carries the Baby Jesus in the Christmas parade."

Amanda went through her childhood itinerary, which was full of twists: her adolescence, her youth, the present. Through her life she had come across so many Bibianas she could no longer recognize them. They had the same face, they all wanted to be the only ones to carry Baby Jesus. He too had changed; lately, he had the appearance of a writer. A smile can serve the same purpose, either to betray or seduce, Amanda had proved it many times. There aren't good or bad men, only winners and losers, and literature was a fratricidal struggle. Amanda took the last drink of her cocktail and laughed heartily: "Raúl is an idiot for putting up with me; Alfonso is an idiot for forgetting me; José is an idiot for looking me up." And she fell asleep.

Laura woke her up.

"Leave me alone," Amanda shouted.

"Is it true about Irma, Amanda?"

"I tell you, leave me alone!"
"But Irma is your best friend."
"Go to hell!"

Page 36
He was dark, really he was just common, but he made me feel secure. I was insecure and this made him feel superior to me. Now I congratulate myself for not marrying Alfonso. He was only looking for someone inferior in order to survive.

"Amanda, Irma wants to see you and explain to you."
"There's nothing to explain."
"She insists on talking with you."
"It's not necessary, Laura, I too have cheated and offended, I've taken advantage of others. Tell her not to worry about me, someone will come and deceive her, offend her, make her cry. . . . We are all the same."

Page 50
I don't know if I love him. Our courtship has lasted in spite of my love for Alfonso and in spite of José's intentions. Luis is reliable, a little cold. But does he like me for what I am or for what he would want me to be? I'm in no hurry to get married. In the meantime, perhaps Alfonso will make up his mind. Yesterday he kissed my breasts. . . .

"Each one of us has a place in life. Writing a book is reaching it. Irma wanted to take up two places, usurping mine. Two places . . . we are so insignificant that we go by unnoticed. Irma with her naive face and her ambition of unmeasured recognition." Amanda began to doubt whether she was inside or outside of the book with the blue cover. She hated the woman on the back cover, the characters on pages 36, 50, and 82.

"Amanda? It's Raúl, I want to ask you again for the publisher's address. It's not that I've lost it, it's just that I can't remember where I left it. I'm going to submit my poems, the ones that won a prize and the ones that didn't. What do you think? Well, sorry for taking up your time. Hey, what number did you say?"

Page 82
José called me, my husband answered, and they greeted each other "cordially." Luis did not suspect anything. Then José told me he wanted to see me. I wanted to see him too, even though I pretended not to understand him and wished him a nice trip (he was leaving for Europe that afternoon). His poor wife . . . And me. I've taken the story to its limit, the characters are surpassing me, I'll put an end to it.

"Every time I read the book it seems to want to escape from my hands, it's insatiable, it's not satisfied with the number of pages. Today it threatened to leave me if I didn't add new chapters. You cannot do that, I shouted, squeezing it shut. No? it replied, falling off the bookshelf. It had never scared me so much."

"Mom, do you know the spider song?"

"The spider? Oh, yes, 'Two characters were swinging on a spider web; when they saw the thread was strong, they went to call another one. Three characters were swinging on a spider web; when they saw the thread was strong, they went to call another one. Four characters were swinging on a spider web; when they saw the thread was strong, they went to call another one. Five characters were swinging . . ."

"Are you sure that's how it goes?"

"Positively."

"And the web never breaks?"

"The web?"

"Yes, with so many characters."

"What characters?"

"I'd like to speak with Amanda, please. She's not home again? Tell her Raúl called."

*

"Laura have you seen my book? I don't know where I left it.
What if it was stolen, Laura? I need my book, Laura, Laura. . . ."
"Ma'am, have you seen a book like this? Look, like this, it's
blue, I wrote it. I lost it this morning, no, a year ago, or . . ."
"Sir, have you seen a blue book? I'm on the back, Amanda.
What, don't you know me?"

Page 36
If I don't marry you, I won't marry anyone else.

Page 50
It's about time we got married, everyone gets married.

Page 82
I married her without loving her because you married someone else.

"There are two men who love you; you'll be happy with either one."

"And the third one?" Amanda asked the gipsy. And she began to write the story of her life.

"She cannot find the book, she's certain it abandoned her for not adding more pages to it. She goes out every day to look for it. Raúl came looking for her, he's worried, he wants the address that only Amanda has, he said that it's urgent because today he turns fifty-four."

Epilogue

The day Señora Rodríguez awoke with a tattered purse Señor Rodríguez was particularly pleased. "About time," he exclaimed. He was tired of reading the manuscript entitled *Señora Rodríguez* time and time again and, on arriving at page 125, starting all over again. The only way of resolving this was to switch purses, so he began to discuss with his wife that just the previous afternoon he had seen, in the Puerto de Liverpool, one that he liked because it was . . . Señora Rodríguez did not let him finish, she never expected this from him, she reproached him, clasping her purse with both hands, and asked her husband for a divorce before going to the doctor. After examining the purse for more than ten hours and discovering that the inside was older that the outside, the doctor advised Señora Rodríguez that it be operated upon, in order to stop the disease from spreading to its owner and forcing them to turn her inside out. Furthermore, the purse was already ruined and about to fall apart. Señora Rodríguez did not hesitate: she refused the mutilation. "Your life is in danger," the doctor insisted. Exactly, she responded, and, placing some aspirin in the purse, she went home, lay herself on the bed, and died. When they were about to be buried the purse opened up, allowing the soul of Señora Rodríguez to escape. Señor Rodríguez picked it up, planted it in his garden, and now he has a tree that bears purses full of memories.